Living One-Night Stand

The Loft, Book One

NOELLE ADAMS

One

Jill Armstrong grabbed her bag and keys, closed the front door on her roommates arguing on the couch, and ran downstairs to Tea for Two, the tea shop just below her apartment in Blacksburg, Virginia.

She needed a cup of tea to give her courage for the evening. She was meeting a guy she'd met online, and she'd never done that before. She definitely needed some emotional sustenance in the form of a hot beverage.

The tea shop wasn't crowded at seven on a Saturday evening, so she smiled at Carol Murphy, one of the co-owners of Tea for Two and the fiancée of Jill's boss, and waited as Carol served an older couple their decaf and pastries.

When she stepped up to the counter, Carol said, "You look nice tonight. Do you have a date?"

Jill glanced down at her short, pleated skirt, high boots, and fitted polka-dot blouse, which she'd chosen because the outfit looked a little sexier than she normally wore. She usually dressed in what her friends described as geek-girl chic, and she had no clothes in her closet that looked traditionally stylish. She hadn't even tried for that. If a guy didn't like the way she dressed, then he wasn't going to like her.

She'd come to that conclusion a long time ago.

"Y-yeah. Sort of. Just meeting him for the first time."

"Ooh, did you meet him online?" Carol handed Jill the cup of cinnamon tea she'd ordered.

"Yeah. I figured I'd give it a try. It's been more than a year since Ted dumped me. I'm more than ready to move on. I got a new job. Now it's time for a new man."

"Good for you," Carol said with another smile. She had big gray eyes and the sympathetic, focused expression of someone who really listened and paid attention to other people. Jill liked her and didn't feel the normal awkwardness she would have felt at interacting with her boss's girlfriend.

Carol had actually helped Jill get her current job as a software developer at a small, successful IT company owned by Patrick Stevenson. Jill had been telecommuting with a large company in California, but they'd wanted to move all their staff in-house, so she'd had to either move or find a new job. She'd done her research, discovered Patrick's company was located in Blacksburg, and heard nothing but good things about him and the work they did. Then she'd realized that the cute, quiet guy who was always hanging out in Tea for Two with Carol and her friends was Patrick himself, so she'd asked Carol about possible jobs and had ended up getting one of the new positions he'd created since the company was doing so well.

The whole thing had happened so quickly and easily that Jill could hardly believe it. She'd started her job three months ago, and she loved everything about it so far.

"You don't look too excited about it," Carol added when Jill hadn't replied.

"Oh. Yeah. I'm a little nervous, I guess. It's been a long time since I dated. I was with Ted for four years, and before him I never really dated much at all."

"I felt the same way before I got together with Patrick. The idea of going out on a date was like a visit to the dentist for me. But I'm glad I made myself do it. I bet you will be too."

Jill nodded. "That's what I keep telling myself. I do want a forever relationship and a forever man, and sometimes that means you have to take real steps to get it. So that's what I'm doing." She glanced at her phone and saw the time. "I better get going."

"Come by tomorrow and let me know how it went," Carol said with an encouraging squeeze of her arm. "And try to have fun."

"I will." Jill waved as she left the shop with her tea, and she drank it as she walked to where her car was parked in the lot behind the building.

She was meeting the guy at a trendy bar half a mile away, but she wanted to drive instead of walk, just in case the guy walked her back after they were done.

She didn't want him to know where she lived. Not after a first date.

She had to circle twice before she found a parking place, but she lucked out when a group of teenagers piled into an old Thunderbird and left an empty space. Before she walked into the bar, she stood for a moment, finishing her tea and summoning up her nerve.

She wasn't good at dating. She wasn't good with men. She liked people in general, but when it came to romance, she always became stiff and awkward. She'd kind of fallen into the relationship with Ted during her senior year of college. She'd hoped something similar might happen to her again, but it hadn't.

If she wanted a man, she had to go out and get one.

Squaring her shoulders, she tossed her cup into a trash can before she walked into the bar.

It wasn't very crowded since this was spring-break week at Virginia Tech, so most of the students had left town. There were a few couples scattered around. One group of young women. A middle-aged man sitting alone at a table. And a younger man sitting at the bar.

3

She was quite sure neither of the men sitting alone was the one she'd arranged to meet. One was way too old, and the other was way too good-looking.

In her limited experience with dating, people usually didn't end up looking far better than their pictures, and the guy at the bar was what she'd always considered typical-handsome. He had the clean-cut features and lean, strong body that a majority of people found at least somewhat attractive. Even his clothes were typical. Worn jeans and a long-sleeve gray shirt. The guy she'd arranged to meet was more like her—cute in a quirky, unique way.

She walked up to the bar and dropped her bag on the floor so she could heft herself up on the stool. She was very short, and it wasn't easy. Her skirt slid up much farther than was appropriate.

As she awkwardly tried to tug it back down, the good-looking guy at the bar glanced over, giving her a quick once-over or maybe figuring out what her gyrations were about.

He was even better looking than she'd originally thought. Very, very good-looking. Not her type at all, but still...

Although she found the guy's slight five-o'clock shadow, green eyes, and thin, intelligent mouth incredibly sexy, she was quite sure he wasn't her date for tonight.

When she'd managed to get her skirt back in place, she gave the guy a quick smile since he'd obviously caught her checking him out. "You try getting up on one of these stools when you're my height," she said lightly, trying not to feel embarrassed about her skirt debacle the way she was tempted to.

The guy was a stranger. His impression of her didn't matter. At all.

He chuckled and sipped his drink. It looked like whiskey. "I wouldn't even want to try."

She pulled out her phone so he wouldn't think she was looking for a conversation. No messages from her date. It was three minutes after they'd planned to meet, but maybe he was one of those people who was always late.

That wouldn't be a good match for her.

She wasn't too fond of chronic lateness.

When the bartender came over, she asked for a glass of rosé since she didn't want to just sit around doing nothing as she waited.

She glanced over at the handsome guy and saw he was slanting her a look. There was a very obvious glint of amusement in his green eyes.

"Are you laughing about my ordering rosé?" she asked. There was no particular reason for her to suspect that this detail was what had prompted his amusement, but she did suspect.

Evidently she was correct. He chuckled again—a warm, husky sound that was far too sexy to be entirely fair. "It's very pink, isn't it?" He was watching as the bartender slid the glass over to her.

"Yes, it's pink. It's pretty, and I like how it tastes. Rosé gets a bad rap because of guys like you. I could be equally patronizing about that ugly, disgusting stuff in your glass, but I'm not usually an asshole that way."

"It's not disgusting," he said, his lips twitching irrepressibly as he took a swallow of his whiskey. "This is the good stuff."

"I think even the good stuff is undrinkable, and I guarantee most people wouldn't drink it at all if they hadn't been indoctrinated that it was supposed to be good. You can

5

follow the herd and convince yourself you like it all you want. I'm not convinced." She didn't know why she was talking like this with a stranger. She was normally pretty quiet with people she didn't know.

But the guy looked like he was enjoying the conversation, and it was taking her mind off meeting her date.

"I guess you don't follow the herd much, do you?" His eyes were running up and down her body again, lingering on her thighs above her boots and on her cleavage.

Her body was small and curvy—not particularly thin but firm and compact. It was clear he liked how she looked, and she couldn't help but shiver with pleasure at the knowledge.

"I follow the herd if the herd is going somewhere I want to be," she told him honestly. "If it's not, then I let it go on by."

He gave a slow nod. "That's a good philosophy."

They fell into silence as they sipped their drinks, and after a minute Jill glanced down at her phone again. Still no message. And now the guy was very late.

Her hopes for the evening were falling quickly.

"Are you meeting someone?"

"I'm supposed to be," she said. "You're not here to meet someone, are you?" The question was mostly casual since she was still sure he wasn't her date.

He shook his head. "Just killing time. I'm at the hotel next door."

Most of the hotels in and around Blacksburg were chains, but there was one boutique hotel downtown. That must be where he was staying. "You in town on business?"

"Something like that."

She wasn't sure what to make of that answer, but she didn't pursue the topic. If he didn't want to tell her why he was visiting Blacksburg, then that was his concern.

"How late is your date?" he asked.

"More than ten minutes now."

"How long will you give him?"

"I'm about to give up."

"Were you excited about him?"

"Eh," she said with a little shrug. "I'd only connected with him for about a week. I'm not excited enough about him to wait more than fifteen minutes."

"Was it one of those dating apps?" the guy asked.

"Yeah." She sighed. "Maybe he got a look at me and left."

"No chance." His eyes were warm and admiring again. It was very clear he liked how she looked.

She wasn't used to men being quite so open about that kind of interest—mostly because she usually hung out with nerdy types, many of whom were socially awkward like she was. It was a heady feeling—this gorgeous guy thinking she was attractive. Certainly not something that happened to her on a regular basis.

She glanced down at her phone again and then around at the bar, but no one new had come in. "This was the first time meeting someone through the app. Not a good start."

"If he was going to stand you up, it's just as well."

"Yeah." She shook her head. "Story of my life."

"What is?"

"What is what?"

"What's the story of your life?"

"Finally getting the courage up to take a chance and having it blow up in my face."

He chuckled, sliding off his stool and moving two over so he was sitting on the one directly beside her. "I need more detail than that to fully assess your situation."

She blinked. "More detail about what?"

"The story of your life. Tell me about it." He was still relaxed, amused, slightly teasing. He was clearly having a good time without any particular investment in this conversation other than leisurely interest.

Because his attitude was so casual, she felt perfectly comfortable talking to him. She was here with half a glass of wine still to drink. She might as well pass the time in an interesting way. "Well, I'm twenty-six years old, and I've only had one serious boyfriend."

"That's interesting," he murmured, his eyes focused on her face. "But you've skipped too much information. Start from the beginning. What were your parents like?"

"I never knew my dad. And my mom..." She let out a huff of laughter.

"What about your mom?"

She picked up her phone again and searched quickly through the pictures until she'd reached the one she wanted. She passed it over to the guy beside her.

The picture was of her and her mother about fifteen years ago. Her mother wore a broomstick skirt, a loose tank top, and very long, unbrushed hair. Her skin was tanned, and a guitar was leaning against her leg. Jill was in the picture too— blond and serious and wearing glasses and a little pink sundress. Both of them were standing in front of a run-down RV.

"Wow," the man said after studying the photo.

"She's basically an old hippie. She was forty-five when she had me, and she was still wandering the country in her camper, going to concerts and craft fairs and local festivals. We lived in that RV for my entire childhood, and we never stayed anywhere more than two months."

"How did you go to school?"

"She taught me. She's really smart, and I had the equivalent of a high school education by the time I was fifteen. But the only other kids I knew were the ones we happened to run into and a few on the same circuits my mother traveled in."

"No wonder you've only had one boyfriend," he said, looking genuinely intrigued. "Was it lonely?"

"Sometimes. I love my mother. I always have. And we talked to people everywhere we went. It's not like I wasn't around people. I just never had a real community until I started to connect with people online when I was a teenager. The friends I had online—through games and message boards and fan communities and such—those were the closest friends I'd ever had."

"Did you go to college?"

"Yeah. In California. It was so strange to be in one place for so long, but I really loved it. And that was where I met my boyfriend, the semester before I graduated."

"How did you end up in Blacksburg?"

Jill made a face, realizing now that she'd have to admit something that still embarrassed her. "Ted, my boyfriend, got a job here. So I moved with him."

"What about a job for you?"

"I took a job so I could telecommute. It wasn't the job I wanted, but it was decent enough. And I could do it from anywhere. He was going to grad school here, so... I came with him."

"And he dumped you?"

She nodded, staring down at her wineglass. "Only after I supported him financially through his grad program."

"Shit," the man breathed, shaking his head. "What a jackass."

"Yeah. I didn't think he was then, of course. And I'm pretty sure he didn't do it on purpose—just use me to live off of while he finished school. But still... I feel pretty stupid about it."

"Were there any signs?"

No one had ever asked her something like that before, and she had to think before she answered. "I... I don't know. He was always very sweet with me. He did nice things and gave me a lot of compliments. But when I think back, there was a lot of just assuming I'd do whatever he wanted to do. Of course, I'd moved for him—without any sort of commitment. We'd only been dating five months at that point. Why wouldn't he assume that I'd just go along with whatever worked best for him?"

The guy had leaned forward, as if he were listening intently. But at that he shook his head again. "It sounds like you're being too hard on yourself. You spent your whole childhood moving from place to place, never putting down any roots. It's not surprising that when you thought you had a chance to settle down with someone you loved, you'd take it even if it meant moving all the way across the country."

She reflected on those words, relaxing slightly as they registered. Maybe he was right. Maybe she wasn't as much of an idiot about Ted as she felt most of the time.

"You didn't want to move back to California?" he asked.

"No. Despite the whole Ted debacle, I actually love it here. I made friends—better friends that I've ever had before.

After I broke up with Ted, I moved in with my two best friends. One of them ended up moving out last year, but she's still in town. I really like it here. I don't want to leave. And I got a new job with a company in town, so I plan to stay here for the foreseeable future. I want roots. I want to build the kind of life I want for myself instead of always trailing around in other people's wakes. I found a job I wanted. I'd also like to find a man. A, er, forever man." She was a little self-conscious about the wording, but it was the only way to describe what she was looking for. "That's why I did that dating app thing. I wanted to take some… concrete steps to get what I want in life."

"Sounds perfectly reasonable to me," he said, propping his elbow on the bar and leaning his head on his hand. "Although you know you can have a man without it being forever."

She frowned. "Excuse me?"

He arched his eyebrows.

She couldn't help but giggle at his teasing leer. No man had the right to be quite so sexy. "I can have sex, you mean."

"Yes, you can."

"Is that what you do?"

"Have sex?"

"Sex without a relationship."

"Yes." He raised his glass to swallow down the last of his whiskey. Then he gestured to the bartender to refill his glass and hers.

"Is that all you ever have?"

"Yeah. I'm not into commitments anymore."

"Were you at one time?"

"I was."

She glanced at her phone one more time and saw that her date was thirty minutes late. There was no way she was interested in hooking up with him now when he hadn't even sent her a message about not showing up. She slid her phone into her bag and accepted the new glass of wine the bartender had poured. "All right. So what's the story of your life then?"

He adjusted on his stool, hesitating for a moment. Then he pulled out his phone and pulled up a picture the way she had earlier. He handed it to her. "I'm from Des Moines. This is my family."

She studied the screen of his phone, processing the twenty or so people gathered into the frame. She saw him right away in the back row on the side. There looked to be parents and grandparents and siblings and children.

"How big is your family?"

"I have two brothers and a sister. They're all married, and they all have kids. I'm the youngest."

"And you're not married?"

"No."

"And you have no kids."

"No."

"What do they think of you?"

"They've decided I'm in some sort of early midlife crisis."

"Midlife crisis? How old are you?"

"Twenty-seven."

"Twenty-seven! Why do they think it's a midlife crisis?"

"Because I've spent most of my life doing what everyone else did. Following the herd, like you said. I played sports and got good grades in school. I went to a local university. I got a good, boring job."

"What job?"

His mouth twisted slightly, and he didn't answer.

Genuinely fascinated now, she didn't even think about potentially being rude or pushy. She simply wanted to know more. "What job?"

"CPA. I was an accountant. I got a good job, bought a house in the same neighborhood as my parents, found a woman I thought I liked, and asked her to marry me. My life was... vanilla. For years and years. Nothing but vanilla. I did what everyone expected me to do. I worked hard every day. I followed all the rules. And then..."

"Then what?" she breathed, leaning toward him.

"Then... bam."

She blinked. "What was the bam?"

He shook his head, looking away from her for the first time. "Sometimes something happens that proves to you that the world you're living in isn't the world you want. It... changes everything."

"What happened?"

"It doesn't matter. It changed everything. I didn't want my job, so I quit. I didn't want my house, so I sold it. My fiancée didn't want the man I was turning into, and I wasn't sure I wanted to spend the rest of my life with her anyway, so we broke up. I moved. I started to live my life differently—not doing what anyone expects me to do, just doing what I feel like at any given moment. I don't try to fight the current anymore. I ride the tide. Things happen to you in life. It's easiest to just let them happen."

"You have to support yourself somehow, don't you?"

"Yeah. Sure. I have a lot of savings from years of being a good boy, and I'll still do some work around tax time. But..."
He gave his head another one of those little shakes, like he was

trying to brush something out of his mind. "I'm not going to go into an office every day. And I'm not going to make promises to women that I'm not sure I can follow through on. I'm just going to… ride the tide."

"Wow," she breathed, thinking through his story and wondering what had happened to him to make such a dramatic change in his life. It was clear he wasn't going to tell her, and she wasn't in any position to nag him about it—although she still really wanted to know. "I guess we're kind of in opposite motion then."

"In what way?"

"I'm looking for roots, for stability. And you're trying to tear all your roots out of the ground."

"Yeah. That's exactly right." He held her eyes for a long time, and it was one of those strange moments of bonding that hit you unexpectedly—when all of a sudden you catch a glimpse of someone else's soul. It moved her, took her breath away.

It must have hit him that way too. Or something similar. Because he reached out and put his hand lightly over hers, which was resting on the bar. His fingertips very lightly stroked over her knuckles, and the little touch sent intense shivers all through her body.

"Maybe you should try it," he murmured, a husky texture in his voice that was new.

"Try what?"

"Living for the moment, riding the tide, doing what you want. Just for the night."

Her lips parted. "Are you…"

"I am."

"You're suggesting…"

"I'm suggesting."

"You want us to..."

He leaned closer to her, his green eyes deep and mesmerizing. "Yes, I want us to. But only if you want to too. What do you say? Try to have some fun just for the night."

Never would she have considered going to bed with a man she'd just met like this. She didn't even know his name.

She was a careful person. She had certain things she wanted in life, and she was resolved to make them happen for her.

She didn't ever—ever—ride the tide and let things happen.

But she felt strangely close to him, and he was the sexiest person she'd ever met in her life.

And what would be so wrong about having a little fun, doing something just for her?

His mouth quirked irresistibly just then. "Unless you want to sit around and wait to see if your date is going to show up."

"No. I'm not going to wait for him." She hesitated, and she appreciated the fact that he backed off, waiting for her to make her decision.

She wanted a stable, rooted, settled life, but she also wanted to have fun occasionally.

Why couldn't she branch out a little—do something wild and spontaneous? She wasn't likely to ever meet a man she wanted as much as she wanted this one. She couldn't even imagine anyone as sexy as him.

"All right," she said at last. "Why not?"

Two

When Lucas Bradford had gone to the bar next door to his hotel an hour ago, he'd had no plans to hook up with a woman. He'd just wanted to get out of the room, have a drink, look at something other than the television.

So when the tiny blonde had come in with her big bag and her high boots and her gorgeous body, he'd not set out to make a move on her. He hadn't even planned to talk.

But she was interesting. And genuine. And prettier as each moment passed. And the sudden, unnerving moment of emotional connection they'd experienced had really moved him.

He could usually find a woman to have sex with him when he wanted it, but he couldn't always get his first choice. A lot of women didn't want one-night stands, and a lot of women would never go home with a stranger. He hadn't really expected this one to accept his suggestion, but he couldn't help but ask her.

So his blood was coursing with anticipation as he walked with her over to his hotel and then up to the second floor to his room.

The room was fairly neat—since he'd just gotten there that afternoon and hadn't bothered to unpack—so he led her inside and saw her looking around with that forthright interest she'd shown him earlier.

"How long are you staying?" she asked.

"Just tonight." He was relocating to Blacksburg and was moving into his apartment tomorrow, but he didn't tell her that. That was the good thing about a one-night stand. Details about one's life were unnecessary.

She let her leather bag slip onto the floor, and she asked, "Do you do this a lot?"

"Do what?"

"Ask strange women into your room for sex?"

He chuckled. He liked how direct she was. He liked that she didn't play games. He answered her honestly. "Sometimes. It's the only way I have sex now."

"Have you ever slept with a prostitute?"

He shook his head.

She tucked a strand of hair behind her ear. "Have you ever slept with a man?"

He shook his head again, surprised and curious at the questions.

"How old was the oldest woman you've slept with?"

"Around fifty."

Her eyebrows arched slightly, and Lucas was pleased he'd surprised her. Then she asked, "How young was the youngest?"

"When I was seventeen, I slept with a girl who was sixteen. Since I've been an adult, the youngest was nineteen or twenty. She was in college."

"What was the best sex you've ever had?"

He wondered if she was stalling with questions because she was nervous. He took a step closer to her and replied in a low voice, "I'm assuming it will be tonight."

Instead of responding, she giggled. "Oh, you're good."

He grew still, a bit unnerved by her response.

Her full lips turned up in a flirtatious smile. "What was your bam?"

The question out of context would have been confusing, but he knew exactly what she was asking. She wanted to know what had happened to him. She wanted to know what had changed his life.

He didn't tell anyone. He didn't want to be defined by something he'd had no control over. He didn't like to think about it, remember it. And he suspected that, after he said it out loud, it wouldn't seem as life-changing to another person as it did to him. So he was sincerely surprised when he was on the verge of admitting it to her—for no good reason. He even opened his mouth to begin.

But then he shut it again. A fleeting connection—both emotional and physical—could be enjoyable, but anything more than that was dangerous. There was no reason to invest too much in this encounter since he'd never see her again after tonight.

Lucas had come to Blacksburg for another new start— one in a series of new starts he'd made for himself in the past two years—and he didn't want the bitter truth hanging over him on his very first night here.

Instead of speaking, he shook his head. "Does it matter?"

Her face fell slightly, but she clearly hadn't expected him to tell her. "No. It doesn't. I just wanted to know."

She looked almost irresistible, standing in his hotel room, looking at him with wide blue eyes. Her blond hair was loose and shoulder-length, hanging in slightly tousled waves that appeared natural rather than styled. Her small body was firm and shapely, set off by those sexy boots and the way her top stretched across her breasts. Her eyes and mouth were a little too large for her face, but he liked that about her. Her clothes, her makeup, her whole manner was unique, original, full of personality.

His body started to tighten as his eyes moved from her face to her breasts to her legs and back up again. After their conversation, he wanted more than just her body. He wanted her to give all her bright, sharp spirit to him. He wanted to feel all of it against him in bed.

He took a step closer to her and pulled her into a kiss, tangling the fingers of one hand into her hair. She kind of melted against him, so it was clear she wanted him too. Her body was soft and small and deliciously eager as she pressed against him and opened to his kiss.

He was fully aroused in no time, sliding a hand down to her bottom and pressing her pelvis snugly against him. He was really getting into the kiss, his head roaring with arousal and his body as hard as hard could get, when he felt her withdraw slightly.

First her mouth broke away from the kiss, and then, gasping softly, she took a step back.

He immediately released her, although his stomach dropped with a hard thud of disappointment and his body screamed at him to pull her against him again. "What's the matter?" he asked, as breathless as she was.

"Sorry," she said, making one of those twisting expressions that was somewhere between embarrassment and reluctance. "It was good. I don't know. I don't... know. I just got... nervous or something. I mean, I did... I do want this. It's just that you're a stranger, and..."

She met his eyes, and her expression distracted him from the hot arousal still pulsing through him.

She *was* nervous.

She was a little bit scared.

He let out a rush of air and took a step back from her. "Yeah. Sure. I get it." His dick wasn't at all pleased with what his voice was saying, but he'd never given his dick control of his will, and he wasn't about to start now.

"I'm sorry," she said, her face twisting even more. "I feel like an idiot."

"You shouldn't. You don't know me. And I know there are guys who... You don't know me. You can leave. Right now if you want. Or we can go somewhere else—back to the bar or something—and just..." He didn't finish the sentence since he assumed she would simply walk out.

He wouldn't blame her. There were a lot of assholes out there. And some guys who were worse than assholes. Even a cursory glance at the news over the past year would prove how true that was. She would have no way of knowing if he was one of those men. Not from an hour's worth of conversation and one (very hot) kiss.

He'd have to go find the workout room in this hotel and run hard on a treadmill for about two hours to work off all the tension after she left, but he wouldn't blame her for not making herself completely vulnerable to a man she didn't know.

He wouldn't blame her at all.

She stared down at the floor and threaded her fingers together in a restless gesture. "Okay, now maybe I don't want to go."

"Really?" he asked with a jerk of his head.

With a nervous giggle, she said, "You should see your face."

"What? Did I look kind of excited?" he asked dryly, feeling strangely self-conscious. He'd had a lot of one-night stands before, and in not one of them had he felt like this. Slightly insecure, as if he were treading new territory just as she was.

"A little. I really don't mean to be wishy-washy, but I don't feel nervous anymore. So maybe…"

He could see that she was still torn, and no matter how much he wanted to have sex with her, he didn't want to have sex unless she wanted it as much as he did. He cleared his throat and said, "I don't think you're being wishy-washy. I think you're trying to decide what you want. If you want to do this, we could figure out a way to make sure you're comfortable. What about if you take control of it? You could decide what we do and when. Or if you need more time, do you want to go get another drink while you decide? Or, no, maybe not a drink. We could get dessert or something. We don't have to stay in this room." He was rambling on, and he felt stupid about it, but he was doing his best.

She stared at him for a minute, her expression soft, almost awed.

He stared back at her, wondering how he'd stumbled on doing the right thing for once in his life.

That look in her eyes…

His dick was howling at him in protest, but he ignored it, as any decent human being would.

He'd do a lot more than be a decent human being to prompt that look in her eyes.

"All right," she said softly. "Let's go get some dessert while I decide."

He smiled at her, and she smiled back, and when he walked over, she took his arm as they turned toward the door.

They'd gotten as far as where she'd dropped her bag when she suddenly turned to face him.

"All right," she said in a different tone. "I've made up my mind."

He gazed down at her, momentarily disoriented.

His mind cleared quickly enough when she reached up to pull his head down into a kiss.

He kissed her urgently since his body had immediately leaped back into action, but after a minute he asked against her mouth, "Are you sure?"

"Yeah. I'm sure."

"Fuck, am I glad to hear that."

She laughed against his mouth as he pressed her body against his again. His erection was pulsing in hard throbs, the hot desire rippling out to saturate his whole body. She felt so small against him. Small and soft and incredible. Both his hands went down to cup her bottom.

He couldn't believe he was allowed to touch her like this. He couldn't seem to stop.

"Did you mean what you said?" she asked, pulling out of the kiss briefly.

"Probably. What did I say?" His mind was a heated blur now, so he hoped he hadn't missed an obvious thread of the conversation.

"About letting me have control?" Her blue eyes were big and questioning.

"Yes. I meant it. We can definitely do that. Did you like that idea?"

"Kind of."

For some reason he was getting more excited than ever. Her expression was slightly shy and slightly naughty, and it was the sexiest thing he'd ever seen. Reminding himself that he had to follow through with what he said, he dropped his hands to his sides and said, "Your call then. Tell me what to do."

She was smiling, but then she glanced from the bed to him and then back to the bed. "I hope you're not expecting anything very creative. I don't know that I'm very exciting in bed."

"I don't believe that for a minute." He could see that she was a little self-conscious about getting them started, so he said with a lilt in his voice, "If I were in control, I might start by getting rid of some of our clothes."

"Ah. Good idea." She looked relieved to have something constructive to start with, and she gave him a flirtatious smile as she leaned down to unzip her boots. She wore some sort of socks beneath them—longer than knee socks, black with quirky little pink bows on the tops. She kept those on (a fact that gave him a little thrill) and then unzipped her skirt and let it fall to the floor.

She had little pink underwear on, and Lucas's whole body gave a swell of desire at the sight of her rounded hips, shapely thighs, and bare skin. Slowly she unbuttoned her top, and he was almost leaning forward, trying to catch a glimpse of the fair skin revealed as she pulled the fabric apart. Her pink bra matched her panties. Her breasts were full and firm, and his erection was so tight in his jeans he was momentarily afraid he was going to lose control.

As she dropped her top to the floor, she made an exaggerated stripper pose and sang, "Boom chicka mow mow."

He burst into surprised laughter and almost stepped toward her to scoop her up and lift her onto the bed when he remembered she got to call the shots.

"Now you can get rid of some of your clothes," she said.

He had his shirt, jeans, shoes, and socks off in about two seconds, and he didn't even care that she was laughing helplessly at his speed. "Were you expecting more of a stripper routine?" he asked, his voice hoarse because it was taking a genuine struggle to keep himself from touching her.

She shook her head. "I'm not really into strippers." Her eyes were running up and down his body, and as far as he could tell, she liked what she saw. He wore nothing but a pair of gray boxer briefs, and her gaze lingered on his groin, where his erection was clearly evident. "Okay," she said after a moment.

"Okay what?"

"Okay. You can... get over here and do your thing."

"What thing?" He was asking for clarity, even as he took four strides over to where she stood.

"Whatever you do. It's going to get tedious if I have to narrate everything. Just, you know, kiss me again and then do some stuff you want. I'll tell you if I don't like it."

"You will?" he asked, clenching his hands to hold himself back for a few seconds longer.

"I will." Her expression changed briefly. "You have a condom, don't you?"

"Yeah." To save himself the trouble later, he went over to his suitcase and pulled a strip of condom packets out of a zipper pocket. He put them on one of the nightstands and then moved back to stand in front of her.

Her expression was excited now, heated in a way that went right to his groin. "Okay. Do your thing," she whispered.

Slowly he reached out and brushed a hand down her hair, gently pushing it behind her shoulder. Then he cupped the back of her head with that hand and leaned down into a kiss.

He had vague thoughts about going slow, but it didn't happen that way. As soon as his lips touched hers, his body burst into demanding urgency after having waited so long for this.

His tongue slid into her mouth, and he made a throaty sound as she softened against him, surrendering herself to the kiss. It wasn't long before both his hands were sliding down to her butt and he was lifting her up so their bodies were better aligned.

"Is it too soon to get on the bed?" he murmured, his groin throbbing as he pressed it into her.

"No. Bed is good. Now is good." Her arms were wrapped around his neck, and she was grinding herself against him with a shamelessness that was utterly thrilling to him.

He couldn't believe she wanted him as much as he wanted her.

He turned them around and laid her down on the bed, moving over her quickly because he couldn't stand the distance between them. She pulled him into position above her, dragging his head down into another kiss.

The kiss went on for a long time—deep and sensual and aching in its intensity. Eventually, he could barely even think in full sentences. Just her. And bodies. And lips and tongue and hands and skin. And heat. And need. And desperate need.

And her.

She was making little moans into his mouth. Soft, breathless, and uninhibited. He would swear that they were sincere. She was really enjoying this.

Eventually he started to kiss his way down her neck, but then he remembered their deal. He reared up his head, panting like he'd been running a marathon. "Okay if I take off your bra?"

She nodded mutely, flushed and tousled and beautiful.

He unhooked her bra and pulled it away from her skin, staring like a teenager at her naked breasts until he finally leaned down to tease one with his mouth.

Making himself move slower than he really wanted, he took the time to pay her breasts real attention—caressing and suckling until she was arching up from the mattress and clawing at his shoulders and back.

"Oh God, if you don't make me come soon I'm going to lose it," she gasped after a few minutes.

He lifted his head to look down at her, his vision blurring slightly from the depth of his arousal. He couldn't ever remember feeling this way before—lingering on the cusp between desire and completion for so long. It was strangely intoxicating. And torturous at the same time. "How do you want me to—"

"I don't care. Just do it. Make me come. Please, please, please." She was writhing beneath him, digging her fingernails into his shoulder, the sharp pain only adding momentum to his need.

He wasn't sure he could think clearly enough to focus on oral sex at the moment, so he slid a hand under her panties instead, feeling her with his fingers until he was able to open her to his touch. She was very warm, very wet. She whimpered as he stroked her, and her face twisted dramatically as he thumbed her clit.

"Oh, please," she gasped.

He slid one finger and then another inside her, and he experimented until he'd found a rhythm she seemed to like.

He worked her over with his hand, occasionally leaning down to tease her breasts a little with his mouth but mostly unable to look away from the pleasure on her face.

It didn't take long for her body to tighten, for her hips to start pumping against his hand, for her little moans and whimpers to turn into something louder and more urgent.

When she came, it was intense. Her body clamped down hard around his fingers—so hard he had trouble moving them—and her neck arched up as her mouth fell open in a silent cry of release.

The contractions went on for a long time, and he kept stroking her as she came down. When her body finally started to relax, she was mumbling, "Oh, thank you, thank you, thank you."

His mind was a blur of unexpected emotions—on top of the aching tension of his body—and he had no idea what to say. To distract himself, he leaned down to kiss her again, and she seemed to appreciate that. She kissed him back eagerly and ended up pushing him over onto his back.

He blinked up at her, almost groggy from arousal, to see that she was reaching over for the condom.

He tried to think of something clever or sexy to say, but he was mostly repeating desperate mumbles of gratitude in his mind that he was finally going to feel her body all around him, find an answer for his desperate need.

He watched as she ripped open the condom and then thought of something he could do. He managed to get his underwear off in time for her to take his erection in her little hands.

He made a soft, shameless groan as she stroked him, and he was seriously afraid he was going to lose it if that went on too long. Before he could suggest moving on, she was rolling the condom on. Relieved, he checked its placement and position as she lifted herself up onto her knees and slowly slid down her panties.

He could feel his pounding heart in his ears, behind his eyes, in his groin. Unable to stop himself, he reached over for her, pulling her over on top of him so she was straddling his hips.

Together, they aligned her over his erection, and he was able to slowly edge himself in. She was tight and wet and hot, even through the condom, and he groaned helplessly at the feel of her.

She was breathing fast and hard as she leaned over to kiss him again. He couldn't really concentrate on the kiss, but he did his best, rocking his hips up into her since it was physically impossible for him to hold himself still.

"Oh God," she breathed against his lips. "Oh God, this feels so good." She sounded almost surprised.

"Yeah. Oh fuck, yeah." That was the most sophisticated vocabulary he was capable of at the moment. His hands were gripping her soft hips, and he had to fight not to take control of their coupling.

She lifted her upper body, repositioning herself over him. She braced herself on his shoulders and started to ride him more intentionally.

He groaned in relief as the friction answered some of his need. He stared up at her jiggling breasts and swaying hair and briefly wondered what he'd ever done to deserve living through this moment, feeling this good.

Her cheeks were very red now, and her face was twisting in the way it had earlier, when he'd made her come. "God, I think I... I think I can come again." Her motion over him had gotten faster, harder, sending ripples of pleasure out from his groin.

"Yeah. Yeah. You can come. Come again." He was holding on to her bottom, keeping her in position so he wouldn't slide out of her with her urgent bouncing.

She made a little sobbing sound and slid a hand down to rub at her clit. Then she was shaking over him, clamping down around him so tightly he gave a choked cry.

"Oh God, that feels so good," she gasped, riding out her climax as she moved over him. "Oh God, I can't believe I came."

His head was roaring now as intensely as his body, and he was thrusting up into her from below in hard, urgent pumps as he finally let himself go. It took a minute for him to let loose the last thread holding himself in check, but the buildup just made the release better, hotter, fuller.

He let out a shameless roar as he fell into climax at last. He jerked beneath her, conscious that she was still moving over him, moving with him, stroking his chest with her hands.

He was limp and exhausted when the pleasure finally worked its way through him, and he was strangely pleased when she fell down on top of him, evidently just as sated as he was.

He couldn't enjoy her soft, hot, relaxed body for long. He could feel himself start to soften, and he groaned as he edged her off him enough to take care of the condom.

She rolled over onto her side as he took care of the condom in the bathroom, and he grabbed his underwear from the bed and pulled them on when he came back into the room.

She was watching him. He couldn't read her expression.

"You want a shirt or something?" he asked since she was crossing her arms in front of her chest.

"Yeah. Thanks."

He found her a clean T-shirt and tossed it over to her. He sat on the side of the bed as she pulled it on.

When he looked at her, she was smiling a little. Relieved, he grinned back. "You want some water?" he asked.

"Definitely."

He grabbed two bottles of water and gave one to her. Then he stretched out on the bed beside her, his body feeling tired and hot and incredibly good. "So what did you think of your one-night stand?" he asked lightly.

He really wanted to know. He wanted her to have enjoyed it as much as he did. But he didn't want to sound too invested in her response.

She twitched her eyebrows at him teasingly. "It was the stuff of daydreams," she said.

He couldn't help but like the sound of that.

"I can't believe that was really me."

"Why not?" he asked, cocking his head as he looked at her. "You're amazing."

"Thanks. You're pretty good yourself. And right now I have absolutely no regrets. You're definitely the man to have a one-night stand with."

For no good reason something bothered him about her words. Not that they weren't sincere—since he was convinced they were. She seemed to really appreciate him.

But it bothered him that she was so sure he could only be one-night-stand material.

She was right. That was all he was. But at the moment the idea nagged at him, enough to get in the way of his physical enjoyment.

"But I'm not sure I'll do this again," she went on.

"Why not?"

"Well, for one thing, I might not have such a good experience with someone else. And for another..." She hesitated.

"What?"

"I had an amazing time. And this isn't at all a complaint. But most of the time, I'll want more than this."

He nodded silently, understanding immediately what she meant.

He didn't blame her for saying it, for feeling it.

His life had changed two years ago, and he wasn't going back.

But sometimes he wanted more too.

Three

To her surprise, Jill actually fell asleep in her one-night stand's hotel room.

She only slept for a couple of hours, but it was more than she would have imagined doing—even after having such a satisfying (and tiring) round of sex with him.

She might feel like she knew him now, but he was still a stranger to her. And falling asleep in a stranger's bed just didn't seem very smart. But it was almost three in the morning when she woke up, groggily trying to figure out where she was, who she was with, and what day it was.

When she'd oriented herself, she became aware of the guy stretched out in bed beside her on his stomach, the sheet covering his lower body and one arm bent and tucked under the pillow.

He really did have a great body. His back was smooth and lean and rippling with nicely developed muscles, and his arms and shoulders were very impressive.

She wasn't used to being with a guy who had a body like that. She'd liked how Ted looked, but he hadn't been sculpted like this guy.

Because his back was fully exposed to her, she saw a number of faint pink lines where she'd clawed at him last night in her excitement. Her cheeks warmed slightly at the sight, this sign of how much she'd enjoyed having sex with him.

Then she noticed for the first time a long, jagged scar running from his shoulder blade all the way down to where the sheet was covering his butt. It was old enough to have faded to white, but there were still traces of pink around the edges—so it obviously wasn't a scar from his childhood.

She hadn't seen it last night. He'd never had his back to her.

The scar looked terrible. She wondered what could have done it.

She wasn't likely to ever know.

After she left this room, she'd never see this guy again.

She still didn't know his name. And he didn't know hers.

She couldn't believe she'd really had a one-night stand.

For a few minutes, when the nerves had hit her, she'd been convinced she was going to walk out on him and not have sex at all.

She was glad she hadn't.

She would never see this guy again, but she'd remember last night for a long time. Maybe for the rest of her life.

She'd never felt like that in bed before—so sexy and adventurous and... strong.

She liked the feeling.

When she found a forever man, she wanted to feel like that in bed with him too. She was going to make sure she did.

It took a few minutes to make herself move, but she finally managed to sit up. She needed to get home. If she stayed here too late, Michelle and Steve would know she'd been out all night. She was normally fairly open with them, but last night felt like a private indulgence, a really good secret.

She didn't want to have to rehash the whole thing with them—at least not right away.

So she made herself sit up, wincing at the soreness between her legs. He hadn't been rough, but they'd been enthusiastic, and her body was definitely feeling it.

When she swung her legs over the side of the bed, she felt the man stirring beside her. Looking over, she saw as he opened his eyes.

"Hey," he mumbled.

"Hey. I'm just leaving."

"You don't have to leave yet." He had really vivid green eyes. They were genuinely beautiful, with tiny laugh lines that softened the edges of his handsomeness. His lashes were thick and dark, and his eyebrows a thick slash above them.

"I need to be getting back. I didn't mean to fall asleep."

"Okay." He blinked a couple of times and then groaned softly as he sat up. He swung his legs over the side of the bed the way she had. "I'll walk you to your car."

"You don't have to. I'm just partway down the block."

"It's late."

"Blacksburg is pretty safe."

"You're really arguing with me about this?" He slanted her a disapproving look.

She chuckled and stood up so she could reach her skirt, which was still tossed on the floor where she'd left it. "Okay. Thanks."

She groaned at the thought of putting on her boots at this hour, but she made herself sit down and do it, zipping them up over the over-the-knee socks she'd never taken off. Then she pulled off the guy's T-shirt and picked up her blouse, realizing as she did that she was missing her bra.

It wasn't on the floor anywhere, so she turned toward the bed. The guy had pulled on his jeans over his underwear, but then he reached over and dug her bra out from under the sheets.

He handed it to her with a little quirk of his lips.

She chuckled again and put it on, not failing to see the way his eyes lingered on her breasts as she did.

"How did you get that scar on your back?" she asked as she buttoned up her little blouse. "I just saw it when you were sleeping."

His face went still for a moment. Then he said casually, "An old injury."

"What injury?"

He arched his eyebrows and said dryly, "It's what I get for being a good boy for too long."

That told her very little except that the scar might be associated with the "bam" he wouldn't tell her about. She wanted to pursue the topic. She wanted to know.

But she had no right to know.

She was just another one in a series of one-night stands for him.

He didn't owe her anything but basic decency, and he'd more than lived up to his end of the bargain.

So she bit back another question and gave him a little smile as she went over to pick up her bag from the floor where she'd left it. "All right. I think I'm mostly dressed."

He was wearing his jeans and had slid on some shoes, but his chest was still bare and his thick hair—just a little too long—was sticking up in all directions. He grabbed his key card from the dresser and opened the door to the room.

They walked out of the building and down the block in silence. When they reached her car, she turned to look up at him. "Hey, thanks. For everything. I had a really good time." She could see her building from where she stood, but one didn't tell a one-night stand where one lived, no matter how nice he was.

"Me too." His eyes were warm and slightly sleepy. "I really did."

"Good. Okay. I... uh, better get going." She felt self-conscious again since this was such a new thing for her, but he was as nice and casual about it as she could have hoped for. She gave him one last smile and then got into her car.

She waved as she pulled out onto the quiet street.

He waved back, and when she glanced into the rearview mirror, he was standing on the sidewalk, still looking in her direction.

She drove around the block and was relieved that he'd gone back inside when she returned to the block. Then she parked her car in the lot behind her building and climbed the stairs to her apartment.

It was quiet when she walked in. Michelle and Steve were obviously asleep in their room, and the other room was empty until the new guy moved in later today.

Feeling like she'd won some sort of victory, she went to her own room, changed into pajamas, and got into bed.

She'd done it.

She'd had a one-night stand.

She'd had a really good time.

And it hadn't had any lingering consequences at all.

~

Much later that morning, Jill was sitting on a stool at the kitchen island in the apartment, texting her mother, drinking coffee, and eating cereal.

Michelle, pretty, brunette, and serious, was sitting on the stool across from her, drinking orange juice and working on her laptop. She was a graduate student in electrical engineering at Tech and spent a good portion of her time working—either from home or from campus.

Steve was stretched out the leather couch with a newspaper on his chest. He still insisted on reading paper newspapers, so they were stuck with a pile of them at the end of the week to recycle. He'd been reading one earlier but now had dozed off. He was wearing orange-and-maroon-plaid flannel pants and a T-shirt with about ten holes in it.

Jill liked Steve a lot, although she'd been worried when he moved in seven months ago. She'd originally gotten this loft apartment with Michelle and Chloe—her two best friends—and it had been the perfect setup since none of them could afford the price of a downtown rental as nice as this. Then Steve had moved in with Michelle when they'd gotten serious in their relationship, and a few months later Chloe had moved out. Jill was still coming to terms with the change in her living situation.

She liked Steve, and she was glad Michelle had a man she loved. But instead of living with two women, she was going to be living with two men and one woman. It was an entirely different setup.

And one of the men she didn't even know.

He was a friend of Steve's from college named Lucas. Steve kept saying he was a nice guy and wouldn't be an annoying roommate, but Jill had no evidence yet of those claims.

She didn't like change—particularly change she wasn't in control of. She liked to feel comfortable and settled. She wished she was still living with Chloe and Michelle.

"You were out late last night," Michelle said, looking up from her laptop for the first time since Jill had gotten up.

"Yeah. You all were in bed when I came in."

"So I guess the date went pretty well?"

"Uh, yeah, not really."

Michelle's brown eyes widened. "It didn't? What happened? You were sure out late for a bad date."

"The guy I was supposed to meet never showed up, but I got to talking with this other guy at the bar."

"Oh really?" Michelle prompted, a sparkle in her eyes.

"Yeah. He's just visiting Blacksburg, so there's no potential there or anything, but I liked him. I had a good time."

Michelle glanced over at Steve, as if to verify he was asleep. Then she asked in a whisper, "Did you do anything more than talk?"

"Maybe. A little." Jill was having trouble not giggling with a bubbling excitement. Maybe it was strange to be proud of herself for having a one-night stand, but she was.

"Ooh. Exciting."

"What did you and Steve do last night?"

Michelle made a face. "I wanted to go out, but Steve was tired, so we just sat around and watched the news."

"I said I'd go out with you," Steve objected from the couch, obviously not as asleep as they'd believed.

"Yeah, and then I'd have had to hear whining the whole time about how tired you were. No thank you."

Steve grumbled something wordless and picked the newspaper up from his chest.

Michelle gave her head a shake and her eyes a roll. Jill tried to suppress a little snicker.

"When is this guy supposed to show up?" Jill asked, her voice loud enough to get Steve's attention.

"I don't know. He said he'd be here this morning sometime. I don't keep tabs on him."

"Is he one of those guys who can't follow a schedule?" Jill asked.

"He was usually on time for class in college, but who knows what he's like now. What does it matter?"

"I like people who are on time."

Michelle laughed at that, and Steve muttered, "I'm sure he'll be glad to know that."

"I'm serious. We don't even know if the guy has a job." Jill briefly wondered if this was more common than she'd known. Guys hanging around without jobs. The guy last night had said he only worked when he felt like it. And now her new roommate was arriving in town with very dubious job prospects.

"I told you before. He's going to give us a check for all six months' rent as soon as he gets here. He's obviously got enough money to live on. Anything else isn't our business." Steve sounded slightly impatient but not genuinely bad-tempered.

Maybe the guy had a trust fund or something. Hopefully he wouldn't be spoiled and entitled and obnoxious.

But if he had that much money, why was he moving into a shared apartment?

Jill sighed loudly and leaned her upper body onto the granite countertop. "Why did Chloe have to move out?"

"It's not her fault she lost her job and had to move back in with her parents." Michelle's voice was sympathetic.

"I know. I don't blame her. But she was a way better roommate than some random guy."

"Lucas is a nice guy," Steve said from behind his newspaper. "You don't even know him. And if you don't end up liking him, he'll be moving out again in six months, and maybe Chloe can move back in then."

"I'm sure he's a nice guy. But he's a guy. And I don't know him."

"You'll get to know him." When his phone chirped, Steven picked it up and glanced at the screen. "Soon. He's on his way up."

Jill put down her coffee cup and glanced at herself. Her hair was a mess, and she wore a pair of pink-and-purple fleece pajamas. Both Michelle and Steve were in their pajamas too though, so there was no reason to be self-conscious.

If he was going to share their apartment, then he'd be seeing her in her pajamas fairly regularly.

She was finishing up her cereal when there was a knock on the door. Steve went to open it, and she heard him say, "Hey, man! You made it!" Then he gave the guy at the door a brief hug.

It wasn't until Steve had moved out of the way and the man had stepped inside that Jill saw who it was.

It wasn't a stranger. It wasn't some random guy whom Steve had gone to college with.

It was the man she'd had sex with last night. The good-looking, smart, funny guy who had been so considerate with her. Her one-night stand, whom she was supposed to never see again.

Standing right there in her apartment.

"Hey, this is Lucas Bradford," Steve said with an easy smile. "This is Michelle, my girlfriend, and Jill, our roommate."

Jill stared at Lucas, trying to wrap her mind around the fact that she'd had sex with her roommate last night and hadn't even known it.

He was clearly surprised too. His eyes met hers, and he looked momentarily stunned.

This wasn't supposed to happen.

There were supposed to be no consequences.

She was supposed to have gotten through last night without any lingering regrets.

And yet here he was. Standing in her apartment.

Not just a one-night stand.

In her life to stay.

~

Lucas had spent the morning thinking about his hot night with the little blonde and vaguely wishing he knew who she was, even though that wasn't something he did.

He couldn't get her out of his mind.

He kept telling himself he might as well enjoy the memory since it wouldn't do any harm. And he still had her in the back of his mind when he went down the street to the apartment building where he was planning to live for the next six months.

At first he was sure his thoughts about the blonde were affecting his vision. He thought he must be imagining her sitting at a stool at the kitchen counter as he stepped inside the apartment.

But a second look confirmed the first.

It was her. Her hair was as tangled as it had been when she'd left his hotel room early that morning, and now she was wearing fuzzy, oversized pajamas that hid any hint of her gorgeous body.

But it was definitely her.

Staring at him like he'd just walked out of her nightmares.

She'd had a good time last night. He was sure of it. Just as good a time as he'd had.

She didn't have to look at him like he was the last person she wanted to see.

He wasn't sure how to handle the situation, but he quickly decided that—since she was here first—he'd let her clue him in on how to behave. So when she got off her chair and walked over to him, sticking out her hand and saying with a stiff smile, "I'm Jill. It's nice to meet you, Lucas," he understood that she wanted to act like they'd never met before.

He was fine with that.

He gave her an easy smile and said, "Nice to meet you too. Thanks for letting me take your empty room."

"It's no problem. We needed a short-term roommate, so it worked out perfectly." That was Michelle, Steve's girlfriend, whose smile was a lot more relaxed than Jill's was. "Do you want some coffee?"

"Sure. Thanks."

He dropped the overnight bag he'd carried up, then walked over to the counter to sit on the stool next to Jill's. She'd returned to her seat and was scraping the bottom of her cereal bowl and occasionally slanting him little looks.

She didn't look angry or annoyed or anything. She looked... stunned and a little defensive.

He could understand. Who wanted their random one-night stand to move in with them? They weren't supposed to ever see each other again.

He accepted the coffee Michelle handed him and looked over at Jill again, trying to keep his gaze casual. She gave him a flustered little smile. "So this is the place. What do you think?"

He glanced around the apartment. There was one big, airy common room with high ceilings, big windows, and exposed brick on the exterior wall. He liked the old hardwood floors and the updated kitchen, separated from the main room by just the big island they were sitting around. "It's nice. I like it. It's not bad rent for a place like this."

"It's high for Blacksburg, but not big-city high. And you can't beat the location." Steve had come over to the kitchen to grab a bottle of water out of the refrigerator. "We're pretty easygoing here, so we only have a few house rules."

Michelle said, "Clean up your own mess. Ask before you eat any food you didn't buy. Keep sex in your own bedroom. And don't be an asshole."

Lucas chuckled, although his eyes had shot over to Jill at the mention of sex. She was resolutely not meeting his eyes. "Sounds reasonable. I can do that."

"Good. I'm sure it will work out fine then," Michelle said. "Do you need some help with your stuff. We'll need to put some clothes on, but then we can help you."

"That would be great. Thanks. I don't have much. Just whatever fits in my car."

Steve and Michelle went into their bedroom to change, and Jill went to the sink to rinse out her bowl and coffee cup.

Lucas lingered, so he was waiting when she turned back around.

She stared up at him with big blue eyes.

"I had no idea," he said softly.

She nodded. "I know. Me either. I thought you were just visiting Blacksburg."

"I never said that."

He could see her thinking back, trying to remember if he'd said so or not. He hadn't. He tried to make a point of not lying even though he told almost no one the whole truth.

Finally she nodded again, as if accepting his words were true. "I guess you didn't. I just assumed."

"Sorry."

"Are you? You look kind of smug."

He wondered if that was true. "I'm not trying to be obnoxious or anything, but it is kind of funny. That we ended up…"

"Roommates," she finished for him. There was a glint of irony in her expression, relaxing her face for the first time since he'd gotten here. "Funny isn't the word I'd use. It was supposed to just be…" She sighed.

"One night. I know. But that hasn't really changed, you know. It's still just a one-night thing. You don't think I'm looking to be your boyfriend, do you?"

"No!" She spoke quickly, obviously sincere. "I know you're not. It just feels a little awkward to me." She took a deep breath and squared her shoulders. "Okay. It will be fine. It just took me by surprise. If it's all right with you, I'd rather the others not know what happened."

"I won't tell them." For no good reason he felt a little disappointed about the idea of acting like what had happened between them had never occurred. There was no reason for that response, of course, so he told himself to be reasonable.

"Okay. Good. Thanks. We'll just pretend the whole thing never happened." She smiled at him, more like her real smile, the one he'd seen a lot last night. "I'll show you your room if you want."

He went with her down a short hallway with four doorways off it. He tried to focus on the apartment, but his eyes lingered on her little round butt in her fuzzy pants.

There was no way he should be attracted to her at the moment—wearing those baggy pajamas—but he was. He definitely still was.

"Michelle and Steve's bedroom and my bedroom have their own bathrooms," she said, looking at him over her shoulder and almost catching him leering at her ass. "Your room is here, and you'll have to use the hall bathroom."

"That's fine," he said. The room was a decent size with two big windows and the same exposed brick on one wall. There was a basic twin-sized bedframe and mattress in one corner.

"Chloe left that bed here, so you can use it if you want to. Or we can move it out. You said all your stuff was in your car? Do you have furniture?"

"No. But I can buy what I need. I'll use the bed if she doesn't mind."

"She said she didn't." Jill pushed her tangled hair back behind her ears. "Okay. The bathroom is just across the hall. It's the only one in the apartment with a bathtub, so Michelle and I sometimes use the tub, if that's okay with you."

"Sure. It's fine with me."

He was looking around, but when he focused back on her, he saw that she'd been peering at him closely. He couldn't help but wonder what she was thinking.

"All right," she said with another smile. "That's it then. I'm going to get dressed. Welcome to the apartment, I guess."

"Thanks," he said, returning her smile. "I guess."

She'd started to leave when she suddenly turned back. "We're going to pretend last night never happened, right?"

"I'll do my best," he told her.

He meant it.

But he had some serious doubts about his ability to forget what had happened with Jill the night before.

Four

On Monday morning, Jill overslept.

She usually had a fairly regular schedule—going to bed by eleven or so on weekdays and getting up promptly at seven. Since she worked just a couple of blocks away from her apartment, she didn't have to leave until five minutes before eight, so she normally had almost an hour to dress, eat breakfast, and get ready for the day.

But on Sunday evening, she hadn't been able to go to sleep. She was still in a weird emotional flurry about her one-night stand becoming her roommate, and she stayed awake half the night thinking about Lucas, trying to figure him out and trying not to replay in her mind having sex with him over and over again.

As a result, she'd only had four hours of sleep, and she'd accidentally hit snooze on her alarm. Three times.

It was seven thirty-five when she finally woke up. As soon as she registered the time, she flew out of bed and ran to the bathroom.

She hated being late. As much as it annoyed her when other people were late, she hated it even more when it was her.

She took a three-minute shower, grabbed an outfit that wouldn't take any effort to pull together—a knee-length A-line dress in a vintage print—and snatched a handful of jewelry that might possibly work with it. She'd barely gotten her shoes on before she was rushing into the kitchen to get some coffee.

Michelle was at the counter with her laptop as she always was, eating cereal and working. But what surprised Jill was finding that Lucas was up too.

He didn't have to work. He didn't have a schedule. He could still be in bed.

But there he was, sitting at the counter with a cup of coffee, putzing on his phone. Wearing nothing but a pair of old sweatpants. His hair was mussed, he needed to shave, and he wasn't wearing a shirt.

So the first thing Jill saw as she came into the kitchen was a whole lot of gorgeous male back and shoulders and arms.

She didn't need to see *that* this morning.

She dumped her pile of jewelry on the counter as she poured herself a cup of coffee.

"Morning," Lucas said, sounding friendly and casual.

What was he even doing up this early?

And why did he have to sound so awake? Awake and masculine. Awake and masculine and sexy.

First thing on a Monday morning.

She did her best to suppress a snarl.

"You're running late," Michelle said, without looking up from her laptop. "Did you oversleep?"

"I don't want to talk about it." Jill was trying to drink her coffee and put on her earrings, bracelets, necklace, and rings at the same time.

Lucas was watching her with laid-back interest in his green eyes.

She tried not to snarl at him again.

His eyebrows went up slightly, and she realized she must not have done a good job at the suppression.

She turned her back to him, reaching into the cupboard for a breakfast bar. She preferred to eat cereal, but she didn't have time this morning. She kept her back to Lucas as she gulped down more of her coffee.

"You missed a button."

She stiffened, glancing over her shoulder to verify that Lucas had been talking to her. "What?"

"You missed a button." He gestured toward her dress. "You want me to get it?"

"I can get it," she gritted out, contorting her arms until she could feel which button on the back of her dress was undone. Discovering it, she stretched her shoulders painfully so she could button it.

When she glanced back over at Lucas, she saw that his mouth was tilted up slightly.

He was laughing at her. Silently but definitely laughing.

She didn't try to hide her snarl this time.

He didn't have to be up and dressed and at work by eight in the morning. He didn't have to sit there in her kitchen, looking smug and gorgeous and amused and irresistibly rumpled when she could barely pull it together.

What kind of malicious turn of fate had made him her roommate at all?

When she'd managed her button, she poured more coffee into her cup and took it with her, grabbing her bag on her way out as she left.

She did remember to mumble out a "See you later," before she closed the door.

It was just the first Monday morning of Lucas living in her apartment.

It was going to be a long six months.

~

On Wednesday evening, Jill was sitting at a table in Tea for Two with Michelle and Chloe when she saw Steve standing outside on the sidewalk, waving to get their attention.

She said, "Michelle," and pointed toward the glass storefront.

Steve and Michelle had a silent conversation made up of hand gestures and facial expressions while Jill laughed in amusement.

"Why won't he just come in and talk to her?" Chloe asked.

Chloe was gorgeous in a wild, artistic way with thick, wavy hair and very dark eyes. She was as loud and dramatic as Jill was quiet and contained. Jill had met both her and Michelle at events on campus she'd attended with Ted shortly after they'd moved to Blacksburg, and the three had been friends ever since.

"He won't ever come into Tea for Two," Jill explained, surprised that Chloe wasn't already familiar with this particular running joke. "Says it's too girly."

"Seriously?" Chloe's eyes were wide.

"Yeah. He's mostly just joking, but he never comes in here."

Michelle had finished her wordless conversation, and Steve disappeared from the sidewalk outside.

"What was that all about?" Chloe asked her.

"He's going to the bookstore. Doesn't know how long he'll be."

"How are things going with you two this week?" Chloe asked in a different tone.

Michelle made a face. "Pretty good, I'd say. We've only argued six or seven times."

Despite the light words, there was an edge to Michelle's tone that worried Jill. Her friend had sounded almost resigned, as if she were so tired she was on the verge of giving up. "You want to talk about it?" she asked.

Michelle shook her head. "Don't have the energy tonight. Let's talk about something easier."

"Let's talk about Lucas!" Chloe exclaimed. "Tell me all about him."

"You met him," Jill said carefully, praying with everything in her soul that Chloe wouldn't have a thing for Lucas. She wasn't sure how she would deal with that.

"Only once and just for a few minutes. I want to know more about him."

"There's not much to know. He doesn't have a job. He just hangs around all day and does not much of anything." Jill was trying to sound uninterested, but she ended up sounding a little bitter.

"He's not bad," Michelle said, shooting Jill a quick look. "He cleans up after himself, and he'll do any favor you ask him. He's a nice guy. I like him."

"But you don't like him, Jill?" Chloe asked, her eyes very sharp, very knowing.

Jill shrugged. "He's okay. I don't know him very well."

"She won't even stay in the same room as him," Michelle put in.

"That's not true!"

"Yes, it is," Michelle said, sipping the last of her Earl Grey. "You don't hang out in the living room anymore. You come home from work and hide in your room."

"It's just been a couple of days." Jill felt defensive because Michelle was absolutely right. She'd been avoiding Lucas as much as possible. It just felt awkward around him, and she didn't know what to do about it.

"Yeah, but you live up there. It's your home. You can't always be on guard just because you don't know him very well."

"I know. I'll get used to it. It's just been a couple of days."

She hadn't told her friends about what had happened with Lucas. She didn't normally keep secrets from them, but it felt like so much, so deep. It was too big for her to talk about, so she'd tried to pack all the feelings up and stuff them into a safe little corner of her mind.

"He's really a nice guy," Michelle said. "Just try to get to know him. I'm sure you'll get comfortable around him soon. As it is, he thinks you don't like him."

Jill's eyes widened. "Did he say something?"

"No, but he notices every time you leave the room. I see him watching you. I guarantee he thinks you don't like him."

"Ooh," Chloe said with a little smile. "That's interesting. He watches her. Is there potential there, do you think?"

"No!" Jill's response was too quick, too sharp. She saw the surprise on her friends' faces. "Sorry. I didn't mean it to sound like that. It's just that there's definitely no potential. He doesn't have a job. He doesn't take life seriously. He just kind of… drifts around. There's no way we could ever be in a relationship."

"No," Michelle agreed. "It doesn't seem like you two would be a good fit."

"Oh well," Chloe said with an exaggerated sigh. "He sure is good-looking though. At least he's a little eye candy."

Despite her mixed feelings for Lucas, Jill immediately bristled at the term. "He's not eye candy. He's not just a hot body. He's a person. A human being."

"I know," Chloe said, her eyebrows arching again. "I didn't mean he wasn't."

Jill groaned and slouched back in her chair. "I'm sorry. I know you didn't mean that. I wasn't intending to attack you. I'm just trying to explain why it feels awkward. He's a man, a real live human being. And he's always there, living in my home."

"Yeah. So that means you need to get to know him. That's the only way you're going to feel comfortable with him."

Michelle was right. Jill knew she was.

But that wasn't the only problem.

The problem was that it felt like Jill already knew Lucas.

She knew him and she really liked him.

And she wanted to have sex with him again.

But she'd meant what she told her friends. There was no real potential for Lucas to become her forever man.

He didn't want to be anyone's forever.

He was her roommate, and that was all he could ever be to her now.

~

Lucas was surprised to discover that he liked having roommates.

He'd accepted Steve's invitation to move in because he'd wanted to move somewhere else—anywhere else—and he always went wherever the tide took him. Steve's was the first offer, so he accepted it. He'd had roommates in college, but since then he'd always lived alone or briefly with Carly, his former fiancée. Having roommates was different. It felt like a step backward in some way.

But at the end of his first week in the apartment, Lucas was realizing that he really liked it.

The apartment itself was big and airy and comfortable. He liked the older features and the updated kitchen and bathrooms. He also liked how fixed up it was—with little touches like prints on the walls, throw blankets on the sofas, a vase that Jill always kept filled with fresh flowers. It wasn't fussy or uncomfortable. It was warm. Soft. He liked to look at it, and he knew Jill was the one who kept it that way.

She liked having a home, and she worked to make the place feel so nice.

Lucas appreciated it—since most of the time now he lived in generic hotels or half-empty studio apartments.

In his first week in Blacksburg, he did the normal things. He bought a few pieces he needed for his bedroom. He found a good gym to join so he could work out every day. And he explored the town and surrounding areas. Blacksburg wasn't a city, but it was a decent-sized town, and because of the university, there were plenty of things to do. The rural mountain counties surrounding it were scenic and offered a lot of hiking and fishing and activities on the New River.

Lucas liked it. He wasn't surprised Jill had decided to settle here after wandering for so much of her life.

But Lucas didn't just like the apartment and the area. He also liked having people around.

It was different to wake up and have people to say hello to and to return to. To have people to chat with at all hours. Steve had been a good friend in college, and he was a still a great guy. He worked really hard but had a fairly relaxed attitude about everything else. And Michelle was smart and serious and the least judgmental person he'd ever met.

And Jill...

Jill didn't seem to want to hang out with him much, and it was bothering him more than it should.

He understood feeling awkward about the fact that they'd had sex and then become roommates. But he'd been going out of his way to make her comfortable, and she still barely said ten words to him at any one time.

They'd had a good time together.

They'd really gotten along on that one night they'd shared.

He was sure they could get along again if she would just give him the chance.

Sure, he spent about half the time imagining her in bed with him, but he hadn't acted on it. He could be a decent guy when he needed to be. He could respect the boundaries she'd set.

She could at least give him the opportunity to prove that.

It bothered him that she was so standoffish.

A lot.

On Friday, he'd wandered around town until he'd found a farmers' market, and he'd bought some good fruits and vegetables. He'd had the urge to cook something—he did like to play around in the kitchen when he wasn't feeling too lazy—so he'd started to experiment with vegetables, pasta, and sausage. He thought he might go out later and try to find a bar that wasn't filled with college students, but it was early yet. Not even seven in the evening.

Jill wasn't home yet.

She usually got home by five thirty or six, so he wondered what was keeping her.

Maybe she had a date.

He didn't like that idea.

At all.

Just because he was resolved to be a decent guy with her didn't mean he wanted her to hook up with some other guy while he was standing here in the kitchen, wondering when she was going to get home.

Michelle and Steve were home and in their bedroom. Probably either arguing or having sex. That was what they seemed to do whenever one or both of them weren't working.

At least they weren't loud about it.

Okay, sometimes they were loud about arguing, but they kept it quiet in bed.

He figured they'd probably come out again in time to have some dinner. They liked when he fixed something. He was a pretty good cook.

Jill would probably like his food too if she bothered to come home.

He realized he was being petty and unreasonable, so he tried to talk himself out of it as he added more cream to the gorgonzola sauce he was making.

He had no claim on Jill. None whatsoever.

And if it felt like he did, that was his problem. Not hers.

She could date or screw or marry any guy she wanted, and he had absolutely no reason to complain.

He almost jumped when he heard a key turning in the lock.

She was home.

He glanced back as she entered, catching her shoulders slumping and her head lowering as she put her bag on the floor where she always kept it. She was wearing a short plaid skirt, her tall boots, and a soft sweater that was very thin and very tight. If her legs weren't enough of a temptation in that skirt, the sweater pushed it over the top. Her rounded breasts were very clearly outlined by the fitted material.

They looked big and firm and irresistibly soft in that sweater.

Lucas found himself imagining what he would do with those breasts before he realized what he was visualizing. He pushed the thought out of his mind and said, "Hey there. You okay?"

She was still standing there, looking tired and strangely defeated.

He saw what happened. He saw her make herself straighten up. He saw her force a smile on her face. He saw her put on a pose for him rather than acting the way she really felt.

"Yeah," she said in an almost convincing tone. "I'm fine." She walked over to the kitchen area, her eyes taking in his jeans, T-shirt, and bare feet and then the herbs on the cutting board and sauce in the pan. "That looks good."

"Hopefully. Are you hungry?" He saw she was about to decline his offer, so he continued, "I made way too much, and I don't know if Steve and Michelle are going to ever come out of their room again."

Jill's blue eyes strayed over to the hallway. "Are they fighting again?"

"They were earlier. Not sure if they still are or not."

"Ah." Jill's cheeks grew slightly pink, and Lucas knew she was thinking about sex.

That knowledge wasn't good for his own attempt to keep his mind on the straight and narrow.

He stirred his sauce and reminded himself he was going to be a nice guy. He wasn't going to be pushy and try to get her into bed again when that wasn't what she wanted.

He was capable of controlling himself. He had sex all the time.

One hot night with her wasn't going to change everything.

When she hefted herself up onto a stool at the counter, he was ridiculously pleased. It seemed like she was actually going to hang out with him tonight.

"Bad day at work?" he asked lightly, noticing again that when she thought he wasn't looking, her eyes were heavy and her expression was tired.

"Eh."

"What does eh mean?"

"It means... eh."

"Does that mean work was eh or your desire to talk to me about it is eh?" He'd bought a bottle of red wine from a local vineyard at the farmers' market, and he picked it up, starting to hunt for a corkscrew in the drawers.

"It's in the one by the refrigerator," Jill told him.

He turned around, opened the drawer, and found the corkscrew. Jill reached beneath her for two wineglasses that were hanging on hooks above the wine rack built into the island.

As he poured the wine out, he prompted, "You never answered my question."

Jill was silent for a minute until she accepted the glass of wine he offered her. After taking a sip, she said, "I guess both. Work was eh. Telling you about it is eh."

"I thought we got along pretty well. Before, I mean." He spoke as lightly as he could, although he was seriously invested in her response.

Far too invested. It triggered little alarm bells in the back of his mind.

Being invested meant he was vulnerable.

Being vulnerable meant he was weak.

Being weak meant he got hurt.

"I know," Jill said softly. "We did get along."

"But?"

She opened her mouth. Closed again. Then said, slightly hoarse, "I keep thinking about you and sex."

He was briefly surprised she was so direct, so honest. Then he realized he shouldn't be surprised. That was her nature. Hiding from him the way she'd been this week wasn't.

"What's wrong with that?" he asked, trying to keep the edge of heat out of his voice but not entirely succeeding.

Her cheeks flushed again, more deeply this time, and she dropped her eyes as she sipped her wine. "You know what's wrong with that. We don't... we don't want the same things."

She was right. She was entirely right.

She wanted a forever man. She wanted a long-term relationship, and he didn't.

He really didn't.

He could never be a forever man.

He felt an intense kick of disappointment at that acknowledgment, and his voice reflected it as he replied, "No. I guess we don't."

"So it wouldn't be smart for us to have sex again, but it's hard for me to... to not think about it."

He was glad he wasn't the only one whose thoughts kept going astray. "Yeah. I know the feeling."

Her eyes darted up and then back down, and she blushed even more.

He took a deep breath, pushing past the sudden urge to grab her, kiss her, take her hard and fast right there against the counter. "We had a lot to say to each other before we got into bed. So maybe we could still... talk to each other."

This time when her eyes lifted, she held his gaze. "I'd like to."

"So why don't we try?" He took a deep breath and forced himself past another wave of resistance. He was here for six months, and this tension was going to get old if they didn't take care of it. "I promise not to touch to you again... unless you want me to."

He couldn't help but add the last part since something inside him howled in outrage at the finality of his promise.

He wanted to touch her again. Of course he did.

But he also really liked her.

He might be able to seduce her back into bed—he was pretty sure he could—but that wasn't what she really wanted. And it definitely wasn't worth the angst that would follow if they fell into bed with different goals in mind.

"So you want to... to be friends?" Her expression was genuine, almost hopeful.

He nodded. He wanted a lot more than that, but life didn't offer what you really wanted. He'd learned that a long time ago. Better to just go with the flow, ride the tide, let things happen to you. This was happening now, so he let it. "Yeah. If that's okay with you."

"I'd like that." She smiled at him. "I'm sure eventually I'll stop thinking about having sex with you."

He almost choked in his effort to hold back the loaded comment he wanted to make in response. Then he remembered his sauce, so he turned back to the cooktop, glad for the distraction.

He'd gotten himself together with a firm, mental lecture about controlling his ridiculous lust when he turned back to pick up his glass of wine and smile at her. "Friends it is. No touching. No talk about sex."

His heart gave a silly little skip when she smiled back at him, and he felt a low rumble of that down-deep anxiety.

Why was he feeling this way?

Why was he acting this way?

He'd turned a corner in his life two years ago, and now he was on a different road.

He didn't act... earnest. Not anymore.

He cleared his throat, sipped his wine, and turned back to his sauce. "So what was happening with work today?"

"It wasn't anything terrible. We're just on this big rush project, and I'm not sure how we'll get it done in time. Everyone's all stressed out and snipping at each other, and my boss..." She sighed.

"Your boss what?"

"He doesn't seem... happy with me. Because I can't keep up with these deadlines. I've only worked there a few months, and I don't want him to have a bad impression of me so soon."

Lucas frowned. "I can't believe you're slacking or anything."

"I'm not! I'm working my ass off."

"Then if you can't meet the deadlines, then they must not be realistic deadlines."

"They're not," she admitted. "They're crazy. I don't think anyone could meet them."

"Then it's his problem. Not yours. Is he really an asshole like that?"

"No, he's not an asshole. He's usually a pretty nice guy. But he's just... I don't know... driven. He gets focused on something, and that's the only thing that matters. His sister—she manages the office—she's been telling him to back off and be more realistic about what we're capable of doing. But I don't want to disappoint him. If he wants me to meet these deadlines, then that's what I want to do."

Lucas shook his head, checking to make sure the pasta was done before draining it. "You can't work yourself into a heart attack to please an unreasonable boss."

"He's not—"

"If his expectations are impossible, then he needs to change his expectations. He needs to change. Not you."

She gave him a tired smile. "Yeah. That makes perfectly good sense logically."

"But..."

"But it's not always that easy to make yourself do it. Not when you want to do a good job."

"You are doing a good job. Aren't you?"

"I don't know."

"Yes, you do."

She made a face at him, as if she were briefly annoyed by his pushing. Then she admitted, "Yeah. I'm doing a good job."

"So what's your problem?"

"My problem is I don't like people to be disappointed in me. Especially people I like and respect as much as my boss."

"I told you it was his prob—"

"I know what you said," she interrupted, a kind of fierceness to her tone that he liked. "And I get that you don't give a crap about people's expectations for you. But I do. Even if those expectations are unreasonable, I care about them."

He stared at her for a moment, their gaze strangely deep. It felt like he understood her in a profound way and that she understood him too.

Then he broke the gaze. "You're going to have some of this, aren't you?" he asked, gesturing to the cooktop.

Her lips wobbled irrepressibly. "I'm not sure how I can say no now, after I've been sitting here smelling it for the past ten minutes. I didn't know you were such a good cook."

He felt a foolish swell of pleasure at her words. But his voice was dry when he said, "You better taste it before you start handing out compliments."

The pasta turned out really well. They ate together at the island, having a second glass of wine. After a while, Steven and Michelle emerged, and they had some pasta too.

They hung out there in the kitchen for a long time, and Lucas forgot that he'd been planning to go out and find a bar that evening.

He didn't end up going out at all.

~

By Sunday afternoon, Jill stopped putting on an act and keeping her distance just because Lucas was living with her.

For the whole first week, that was how she'd felt. Like she was putting on an act. Like she had to think about what she was doing, how she looked, how she sounded, because he was watching her.

But it was too hard. It wasn't her nature. And it made her stressed out in her own home. Her friends had been right. She needed to get to know him as her roommate. After their dinner on Friday, she felt better about him, about everything.

And by Sunday she let down her defenses.

This was her real life. Her home. She had to live in it, with or without Lucas Bradford.

She worked most of the day on Saturday, trying to catch up on some of her deadlines, but she knew she couldn't work on Sunday or she'd be exhausted and bleary-eyed at the beginning of the new week.

So she slept in late, had breakfast, then asked Lucas if she could use the tub in the hall bathroom so she could take a bath.

He was on his way to work out—the man was some kind of machine, going to the gym almost every day—so he didn't care if she used the tub. She had a long, leisurely soak, and then went to do some errands and have lunch with Michelle and Chloe.

She was feeling good when she came home. She wanted to hang out in the living room and watch TV, but Lucas was already there. Her first instinct was to go hide in her room, but she fought against it. Instead, she got her nail file and polish and brought them into the living room.

Lucas was stretched out on one of the couches. He'd showered after working out and was now wearing sweats and a worn Hawkeyes T-shirt. He had a sports channel on the television, but he didn't appear to be watching it.

He appeared to be asleep.

She sat down in the big chair and realized he wasn't asleep when he glanced over at her.

"Are you watching this?" she asked, gesturing at the TV.

"Nah. Change it to whatever you want."

Relieved that he was easygoing about the television, she switched over to a cooking channel.

She liked to watch cooking shows on Sunday afternoons.

He appeared perfectly amenable to that, and his eyes focused on the celebrity chef who was making some sort of towering sandwich on the screen.

Jill started working on her nails.

Lucas was still stretched out on the couch—his body lean and hard and undeniably gorgeous, even in his sloppy clothes—and his eyes moved between the television and her work on her nails.

"Do you do your fingernails every Sunday?" he asked. He didn't appear to be teasing. He seemed genuinely curious.

"Usually."

"Don't a lot of women go to have them done somewhere?"

He'd been engaged, she remembered. She wondered what that woman had been like. She thought it was cute he was still pretty clueless about things like manicures. "Some women do. I like to do mine myself. I like to make them pretty." She glanced over at him, wondering if he thought she was silly. "I like to make… things pretty."

"You fixed up the apartment real nice."

She flushed slightly since Lucas appeared to really mean it. "It wasn't all me."

"You'll never convince me that Michelle and Steve did much to fix this place up."

"No. Certainly not Steve. But Michelle, Chloe, and I fixed it up together when we first moved in here. We got all the main furniture and stuff."

"You're the one who keeps it looking so nice though. I've been here a week, and I do have eyes in my head, you know."

She smiled at him. "I like things to look pretty. Homey. You know?"

"Yeah. I know you do."

There was a strange resonance in his tone, and she couldn't quite understand it. He wasn't judging her though, so she didn't let it bother her.

They sat in silence for a while, watching the cooking show. In a commercial break, Lucas said, "I haven't seen Steve all day."

"He and Michelle got into another fight this morning, and he left. I think he's just hanging out on campus."

Lucas gave his head a little shake. "Have they always fought this much?"

"No. They were all lovey-dovey at first. It's just been the past couple of months."

"Are they going to make it, do you think?"

Jill felt a little twist in her chest, the way she always did when she thought about the possibility of Michelle and Steve breaking up.

She hadn't really wanted Steve to move in when he had, but she loved him now. He felt like family. Michelle was one of her best friends though, so Jill's loyalty would always be first with her.

It was going to be so hard—if Michelle and Steve broke up.

She really hoped they wouldn't.

"Is it that bad?" Lucas asked, evidently reading something in her face.

"I don't know. They're fighting a lot. Michelle seems to be getting really... tired. I don't know." She swallowed hard, focusing her anxiety on making her pinkie nail perfect. "I hope they'll figure things out."

"What's the main problem with them? Do you know?"

"There's not one main thing, at least as far as I can tell. Steve is really stressed out at work, and he doesn't want to do anything else when he's not working. But I don't think that would be enough to... I don't know. It was different last year, before Steve got his PhD. When they were both grad students, it was different. They had more flexible schedules and—I don't know—they seemed more in sync." She finished her hand and waved it around to dry the polish. "They fell really fast. They met and were practically living together in less than a month. So maybe it's just normal life stuff—catching up to them."

Lucas was looking at her from the couch.

She added softly, "I don't want them to break up."

"I guess that would blow a hole into your nice settled life here."

She sucked in a breath but then saw that his eyes were gentle. He wasn't mocking her.

"I wasn't just thinking about myself."

"I know you weren't. But they're your friends. It would affect you. Obviously."

"Yeah." She pulled off her thick socks and started on her toes.

She worked for a while, and when she glanced up, she saw Lucas was still watching her. Her hair was in braids, and she was wearing purple leggings with books on them and an oversized T-shirt. He wasn't likely to be leering at her when she looked like this, so it was unnerving that he was still watching her.

"What?" she asked, meeting his eyes.

"Nothing. Just watching the toenail progress." He gave her a lazy smile.

"Don't you get bored?"

"What? On a Sunday afternoon? Nah."

"Not just right now. Overall. Since you're not really working. Don't you get bored?" She was genuinely curious and made sure her tone didn't come across as judgmental.

"No," he said with another smile, turning onto his side so his whole body was facing her. "I got bored when I worked. I don't get bored now. If something gets old, I stop doing it. I move on."

"You ride the tide. I know." She made a face. "I would get bored. Hanging around and doing nothing."

"I do things."

"You work out. You occasionally cook something. What else do you do?"

"I do what I want when I want to do it. Anything I want." His eyelids were heavy, his expression warm and relaxed. "You should try it."

"No thanks. It's great that you're doing what you want to do, but I wouldn't want to do that myself. I like work. I like having a real home. I like... life. I'm not living for vacation."

His expression flickered slightly.

"I didn't mean to insult you," she said quickly.

"I know you didn't. I wasn't insulted. I get what you're saying."

She sighed as she inspected her toenails. "My mom was kind of like you. Always moving. Never wanting to get into what she called a rut. But because of that, it always felt like we were drifting, like I didn't have any... any ties to ground me in the world. She never had roots. She still doesn't understand them."

"Is she not happy with your choices?"

"She's happy that I'm happy. At least that's what she says. But I think she's kind of disappointed in me. She thinks I've become part of the establishment and won't ever be free. But I don't want that kind of freedom. It doesn't feel free to me." Jill sighed, wondering how she'd rambled on into this kind of intimate confession on a Sunday afternoon. "She doesn't understand roots."

"I do understand," Lucas said softly.

She met his gaze and held it for a minute.

"I understand roots," he said, almost like he was taking to himself. "I just don't want them."

For no good reason the last words felt like a kick in the heart.

She had to keep reminding herself about who he was and who he wanted to be.

He wasn't like her. He wasn't looking for the same things.

If he had been, he would have been exactly what she wanted in a forever man.

But he wasn't.

And he never would be a forever man.

There was a guy who worked in the office suite below her that she'd been chatting with in the mornings and evenings. He seemed like a nice, stable, fairly cute guy, and he definitely appeared interested in her.

He was the kind of guy she needed to focus on.

Not Lucas.

Never Lucas.

She wasn't foolish enough to believe Lucas was likely to change, and she wasn't needy enough anymore to simply take what was offered when it wasn't what she really wanted.

If things had been different, she would already be crazy about Lucas.

But things weren't different.

And she wasn't.

Five

Two Fridays later, Jill had a date.

Lucas wasn't happy about it either.

They'd been getting along well for the past two weeks, and Lucas was generally happy about his living situation. He'd been training himself to refocus any time sex crossed his mind in her presence, and he'd even been managing about half the time not to imagine having sex with her when he was in his bedroom alone at night.

He'd been as good as he could possibly be, and it would be nice if that meant he would be rewarded.

Instead of rewarded, he had to deal with Jill fluttering around getting ready for her date on Friday evening. Then he had to watch her leave with the guy and brood about what they might be doing.

She hadn't even met this guy online. She knew him from her work building or something. She knew what he looked like. She knew how he acted. And she wanted to go out with him.

The date wasn't likely to be a flop.

The guy had come to pick up Jill at seven, but Lucas had only caught a brief glimpse of him. He'd had long hair and dark-rimmed glasses and a hipster vibe. Jill probably thought he was a good match for her.

She'd probably have a good time.

She'd probably go out with him again.

She'd probably decide she really liked him and make him her boyfriend.

Lucas knew enough to realize things would be better that way—it would be safer for him and dispel a lot of the tension he couldn't help but feel around her—but he didn't like the idea of it.

He didn't like it at all.

After she left the apartment, he left too, going to a bar he'd found last week with a decent bartender and not filled with swarms of college kids. But he didn't have a good time.

He talked to a couple of women, and they had seemed interested in him, but he couldn't muster enough interest or energy to make a move on them.

Eventually he went back home, sitting in front of the television by himself, watching sports and drinking beer and wondering when Jill and her date would come home.

If they came back here and ended up in her bedroom, Lucas wasn't sure what he would do.

Being friends and roommates with Jill was just fine. It was all he could have since he didn't want what she wanted. He could live with that.

But knowing she was having sex with some other guy in this apartment was more than he could live with.

How the hell had he gotten into this situation in the first place?

He usually slept with women and moved on. He liked it that way. He'd have some vague, pleasant memories of his time with them, and it would never trouble him again.

This was different.

This was... hard.

He scowled at the television as he swallowed down the last of his beer.

It was after ten now. Jill and that guy had had more than enough time for drinks and dinner and dessert.

What the hell were they doing?

Lucas was pretty sure he didn't want to know.

He sat with his empty bottle of beer for a few minutes until he heard a key turn in the lock.

Every nerve in his body stiffened to alert as the front door opened and Jill stepped inside.

For a moment he hoped she'd gotten rid of the guy, but she hadn't. He followed her in.

She blinked when she saw him sitting there, and Lucas wondered if she'd expected him to clear out.

He wasn't going to clear out. He lived here. He was allowed to sit on the couch on a Friday evening even if Jill brought home a date.

"Hey," she said, her voice a little fluttery. Not her normal tone. "Hal, this is my roommate, Lucas." She gestured to Lucas. "And this is Hal."

"Hey, Lucas," the guy said. Hal. His name was actually Hal. "Nice to meet you."

"Yeah. You too."

Jill looked between Lucas and Hal and seemed frozen for a moment. She was absolutely gorgeous in an odd little dress made of lace and corduroy with those tall boots on and those same high socks on she'd worn when they had sex.

Lucas loved those socks. They made his body clench with lust.

Why the hell was Jill wearing them for some other guy?

Finally she turned to Hal with a trembly smile that wasn't really like her. "Do you want something to drink?"

"Sure. Thanks." Hal definitely looked like he was eager to stay. He was probably hoping to have Jill and all her blond hair and big eyes and lush curves and gorgeous legs surrounding him in bed.

With a huff, Lucas hauled himself to his feet, fighting a simmering resentment.

And jealousy.

Definitely jealousy.

He carried his empty bottle of beer to the kitchen, dropped it into the recycling, and then opened the refrigerator for another.

He was there just in time to get in Jill's way.

He hadn't planned it, but he wasn't disappointed about it either.

She gave him a covert glare behind the cover of the refrigerator door. He knew how to interpret it. She wanted him to get out of here. She wanted him to leave her alone.

He plopped himself down on a stool at the island with his cold beer and grinned at Hal. "So how was dinner?"

Hal looked slightly taken aback by his overly friendly tone. "Oh. It was fine. What did you think, Jill?"

She offered Hal a beer and then poured a glass of wine for herself. "It was good." She slanted Lucas another look, but he wasn't planning to budge. "We went to an Italian place. They make their own homemade pasta."

"Sounds good." Lucas swallowed down a gulp of beer. "So what do you do, Hal?"

The conversation went on in a similar manner for fifteen minutes, with Lucas asking a lot of questions, Hal trying to answer them, and Jill shooting Lucas increasingly annoyed looks.

Finally Hal finished his beer and cleared his throat. "Well, I guess I better get going."

Lucas couldn't help but feel a surge of satisfaction.

Then he wondered if he was an asshole at heart for being happy about getting rid of the guy when Jill might have liked him.

The thought dampened his pleasure just a little.

Jill walked Hal to the door, and they said a quiet goodbye. Lucas managed not to peer around the corner to see if the guy was kissing her.

When the door finally closed and Jill returned to the kitchen, Lucas let out a breath in relief.

Thank God that guy was gone.

And Jill hadn't gone to bed with him.

"Asshole," Jill hissed, slamming down her wineglass on the counter so hard the liquid slopped out over the rim.

"What did I do?"

"You know exactly what you did." Her cheeks were flushed, and her hair was slightly tousled, and she was wearing those high socks that ended on her gorgeous thighs.

Lucas was hit with a wave of lust so strong it almost knocked him out.

Jill wasn't distracted by any such thing at the moment. She was practically snapping her teeth at him. "You did it on purpose!"

"What did I do?" Lucas knew what he'd done, of course, but he was convinced he had a pretty good case in his defense.

"Oh, stop acting all innocent. You got in the way of my date on purpose."

"What are you talking about? I live here, don't I? Aren't I allowed to watch TV and get a drink from the kitchen?"

"Yes, you're allowed. But you were getting in the way on purpose. Intimidating him with all your fake friendliness and your... your..."

Genuinely curious now, Lucas raised his eyebrows. "My what?"

"All your shoulders and biceps and everything."

Lucas glanced down at himself in surprise. He was wearing a T-shirt that fitted normally. Nothing about his arms or shoulders was unusual or inappropriate. "I'm wearing a shirt."

"I'm not talking about your shirt. I'm talking about..." She waved her hand toward the general vicinity of his torso. "Your shoulders and everything. You're intimidating to a normal guy."

"I am?"

"Oh, stop looking smug. It's just because you don't have anything to do during the day but work out. But you were sitting there with all your man-ness, and you scared him away. You knew what you were doing."

Lucas tried not to smile because she was sincerely angry with him, but he couldn't help but like the way she'd described him.

Man-ness.

"Asshole," she hissed again.

He clearly hadn't hidden his expression very well.

"Stop smirking," she snapped. "I'm serious. You can't do that. If we're going to be roommates, you can't do that again. I'm going to have dates, you know. I'm allowed to bring men home without you hovering around like some sort of alpha-male caveman."

He sobered at the thought of her bringing a lot more men home. And then he was annoyed by the fact that it bothered him so much.

He was supposed to do nothing but casual relationships.

He wasn't sure why nothing felt casual with Jill.

"I wasn't acting like a caveman," he said. "I was perfectly nice to the guy. It's not my fault he's such a wimp that he got scared off by a guy who works out."

Jill made a frustrated sound in her throat. "He's not a wimp."

"Then why did he cut and run over nothing? If he was really into you, he would have stayed."

"He was into me!"

"Clearly not enough to put up with me hanging around."

"Oh, you... you... asshole!"

"You said that before. I get it. You think I'm an asshole. But that doesn't change the fact that I was sitting in a room that I'm allowed to sit in, and Hal's the guy who ran like a rabbit instead of spending the night with you."

She was almost shaking now with anger. She opened her mouth to snap back a response but then closed it suddenly. She turned her back to him, took a few deep breaths, and then walked out of the room.

Lucas didn't like that.

They were in the middle of a perfectly good argument, and she'd just left him hanging.

He followed her to her room, but she closed the door on his face.

"Jill," he said through the door.

"Go away. If I talk to you anymore, I'm going to bite your head off."

Ridiculously, that kind of turned him on.

"Jill," he said again through the closed door.

"I can't talk to you right now. I'm too mad. We can talk in the morning if you can manage to stop being an asshole."

Lucas started to object, but he didn't.

He walked down the hall to his room.

He was all wound up.

All. Wound. Up.

Frustrated and annoyed and turned on and strangely excited.

But there was nothing in the world he could do with the feelings since Jill obviously wasn't going to let him haul her over his shoulder and carry her to bed.

So he went to take a shower instead.

~

The next morning, Lucas got up around eight to discover that Michelle and Steve were still in bed, but Jill was already up, drinking coffee in the kitchen and looking at her phone.

They stared at each other over the kitchen island.

"I'm sorry," he said immediately. He wasn't all wound up anymore. He'd stayed awake for half the night, thinking about what had happened and what it meant. He could see very clearly he had indeed been an asshole. "You were right. I was a jerk."

Her face had been slightly defensive, but it softened at that. "Yeah. You kind of were. I... I know you live here. And you're allowed to be around and do what you want. I know I can't expect you to just disappear because... because I might feel uncomfortable when you're around. But maybe..."

"I won't get in the way on purpose," he said, hating the fact that he was saying it, that he meant it, that it would oblige him to behave better in the future even if that meant he'd have to let some other guy go to bed with Jill.

She let out a breath, looking sleepy and ridiculously pretty in her fuzzy pajamas and messy hair. "Thank you. You're... you're allowed to bring girls home too. If you want."

He wondered if she wanted him to. "I know."

"I'd feel weird about it if you do. I know I would. I'd be kind of... jealous, I think. I'm not trying to be a hypocrite or something. But... but I wouldn't do anything. If you do."

"I know you wouldn't."

She was a better person than him.

No question about it.

He wondered how she would act if he brought home a woman to have sex with.

He wondered if she would feel as outraged and bristly and mind-numbingly jealous as he had.

He hoped so.

But he wasn't likely to test it out anytime soon.

He was sure it would change in the future, but for the moment he had no interest in going to bed with anyone but Jill.

~

That night, Lucas woke up in a cold sweat.

He lay in his dark room, breathing raggedly, his eyes wide open as he stared up at the ceiling.

He was wide awake and terrified.

He hadn't had a dream or a nightmare. Not really. At least not that he could remember. He was just suddenly awake, suddenly in a panic, like two years hadn't passed since his life had been ripped apart.

When he was capable of moving, he got up and went to the bathroom across the hall. He splashed a lot of cold water on his face. Then he peed and splashed more water on his face.

He didn't have PTSD. At least he'd never been diagnosed as having it. Two years ago, he'd had six months of physical therapy and counseling until all the doctors had declared he was fully recovered.

He was recovered.

He just didn't always feel that way.

His family didn't understand why he'd left his old life behind completely after he was declared well again. No one really understood.

Life didn't feel the same to him as it had felt before.

He couldn't take it seriously. He couldn't take anything seriously.

If nothing mattered that much, then everything was easier. Nothing was painfully bad.

And he wouldn't have to be terrified like this again.

He left the bathroom and stood in the hall, wearing nothing but his underwear. He stared at Jill's door, fighting the urge to knock on it, to wake her up, to talk to her.

She would help.

She would make him feel better.

He knew she would.

His heart was still racing, and he was cold deep down. But he would feel better if he could talk to Jill.

But that would mean telling her everything.

She wouldn't understand either.

She would think he was overreacting. She'd blown up his bam in her mind to such an extent that she would be shocked to hear what it really was.

She thought he'd been a victim of a crime or another similar circumstance. She thought his bam was something horrifying like that.

It wasn't.

It was just one of those things. Something that could have happened to anyone, anywhere.

That made it worse to Lucas. Not better. But no one would really understand that either.

He had no idea how long he stood in the hall, trying to catch his breath, staring at the closed door to Jill's bedroom.

Finally he turned around and went back into his room.

He got back into bed, but it was a long time before he was able to go back to sleep.

~

Jill went out with Hal a couple more times in the next few weeks, but she wasn't as excited about him as she should be.

She didn't even get excited about kissing him.

She wasn't anywhere close to wanting to sleep with him.

And she couldn't help but blame Lucas.

A little.

If he wasn't so ridiculously hot, she wouldn't be always comparing other guys to him.

And if he wasn't so good at sex, she wouldn't be afraid that no other man would ever measure up.

And if he wasn't so clever and funny and thoughtful and (sometimes) considerate, she wouldn't like to hang around him as much as she did.

If he wasn't her roommate, he wouldn't be around all the time.

But after three weeks, Hal stopped calling her, and she wasn't even that disappointed.

For a week after her last date with him, she tried to focus on work—since the big stressful project she'd been working on was finally wrapping up—and not stew too much about Lucas or how he'd hindered her romantic prospects simply by existing.

On the Friday she handed over the project at last, she was relieved and exhausted, and she planned to have a leisurely evening at home. She got takeout from a Chinese restaurant—enough to share if anyone else was around—and bought a good bottle of wine. She even stopped at Tea for Two and bought a box of Carol's cookies.

She was in a pretty good mood as she entered the apartment.

Only to discover that Michelle and Steve were shouting at each other at the top of their lungs.

Jill wasn't big on conflict. She liked things cozy. She liked people to get along.

And she certainly wasn't prepared to be met with a screaming fight as soon as she walked in the door.

She had no idea what the fight was about. They were long past the substance of the argument and were into general denunciations of the other's wickedness.

They paused briefly when they saw her, and Michelle whispered, "Sorry," as Jill went into the kitchen to put down her stuff.

But as soon as Jill made it to the hallway, Michelle and Steve were shouting again.

She had no idea where they got the energy.

Her one somewhat passionate argument with Lucas had lasted about two minutes, and she'd had to flee to her room immediately so he wouldn't see her burst into tears.

When she reached her doorway, Lucas's door swung open and he looked at her across the threshold.

"You want to get out of here?" he murmured.

"Yes," she said, her voice breaking in relief at the idea of doing something other than staying here and listening to her friends fight. "Please."

She ran to use the bathroom quickly, but she didn't bother to change clothes. So in two minutes she and Lucas were leaving, and Jill let out a breath when she could no longer hear the fight.

"You want some dinner?" Lucas asked, peering at her face.

She felt unreasonably shaky, but she tried to smile. "I guess. I'd brought home Chinese, but..."

"The Chinese will save for tomorrow. I'm hungry. Let's go ahead and eat."

She nodded, and after a brief discussion, they walked about a mile to a fairly new shopping center where there was a restaurant that made really good pizza.

They got a table, and Lucas ordered a bottle of wine, and Jill slumped back in her chair.

"You okay?" he asked softly.

"Yeah." She smiled at him again, feeling better, partly because he was being so nice. "I'm just not really used to loud conflict like that. My mom and I never fought. We occasionally snipped at each other but nothing more than that. And I'm worried about Michelle not being happy. And I'm kind of upset about Steve having to move out eventually. And I'm..."

To her embarrassment, a single tear slid down her cheek.

"Sorry," she mumbled, swiping it away. "I'm just not good with conflict. And I'm so, so tired."

"Did you get your big project all finished up today like you planned?"

"Yeah. All done. And I met the important deadline, so Patrick was happy. He said I did a good job."

"Of course you did."

"And he even apologized for being too grumpy."

Lucas gave a huff of amusement. "Did he?"

"Yeah. I think Emma, his sister, made him. But still... I feel better about everything. And thank God that project is done."

The server came with the wine, so they paused for a minute to get their glasses filled and then give their order. Jill couldn't decide between two different kinds, so Lucas ordered both.

The wine was good. Really good. Her eyebrows arched as she tasted it. "How expensive is this stuff?" she asked.

"Eh. Not too bad. I do like it though."

"Me too. Are you sure it's not too expensive? You don't have a job, you know."

He narrowed his eyes at her. "I'm fine. It's not too expensive. And you deserve a little celebration after getting through that project."

She smiled at him.

She must be really tired because the wine was already going to her head.

She drank some more.

And she kept smiling.

~

Two and a half hours later, they were on their way back to the apartment.

They'd finished their bottle of wine, and then Lucas had bought another one. Jill had drunk way too much. She'd also eaten a lot, and Lucas had topped it all off with ordering a chocolate brownie dessert.

All in all, Jill was flying high.

And having trouble walking in a straight line.

Lucas had his arm around her as they walked, most likely to keep her from wandering off into the street. But she liked how it felt. He was big and hard and strong. He had those amazing shoulders, those lovely, toned arms. She liked how his arm felt around her waist.

Like he was taking care of her.

She was giggling over something. It had been a full minute since Lucas had said whatever he'd said that she'd thought was funny, and she really couldn't remember what it was anymore. But she was still giggling about it.

The evening air was cool and crisp and lovely against her hot skin.

And Lucas had his arm around her.

"I wonder if Michelle and Steve are still fighting," she said after a while, deciding it was time for her to say something.

"Surely they've petered out by now."

"Maybe. They might be having sex. They have sex a lot after they fight." She wasn't sure why she'd said that. It wasn't something she talked about—certainly not with Lucas.

"Yeah. Hopefully, they're done with that part too and things are quiet again."

She gazed up at him with blurry eyes. "Do you ever have sex after you fight?"

He blinked. He'd had a lot to drink too, but he wasn't in the same condition she was. She knew it. He was in control. She was buzzed enough for that fact to bother her.

She wanted Lucas to be flying just as high as she was.

"It depends on who I fight with," he said dryly, after a brief hesitation.

"Oh. You don't have sex with me after we fight."

"We don't fight that much."

That was true. Lucas was a pretty nice guy most of the time, when he wasn't being an asshole.

"Oh. We can fight more if you want." This comment made perfect sense in her mind, but she frowned afterward, trying to figure out if that was really what she'd wanted to say.

Lucas chuckled and shifted his arm since she'd started drifting toward the curb. "Fighting with you isn't one of my aspirations."

"Oh."

He tilted his head down and studied her face. "Are you disappointed by that?"

"No. I don't want to fight with you either."

She didn't want to fight.

She wanted to have sex.

And somehow in her fuzzy mind she'd connected fighting and sex.

She thought about that conundrum for a long time until she realized they were standing in front of the door that led up to their place. "We're here," she said.

"Yep." His green eyes were so vivid, so pretty, so warm and strangely soft.

She liked them so much.

"I liked tonight," she told him.

"Me too." He lifted a hand and used it to gently brush a piece of hair out of her face.

She appreciated the gesture since the hair had been tickling her.

"Thank you for taking me out," she told him as serious as she could make herself at the moment.

"You're welcome."

"Okay. I'm going up now."

"All right." He paused. "Is it all right if I come up too?"

"Oh." She had to blink several times and take a deep breath before she worked out that he lived in her apartment the same as she did. Of course he needed to come up. "Yes," she said, pleased she was able to extend such grace. "You can come up. You might need to help me up the stairs. I think…"

"You think what?"

"I think…" She whispered the truth to him. "I think I might be just a little bit drunk."

He laughed, and she liked the sound of it. She wanted him to laugh again. But first she had to make it up the stairs, and it wasn't an easy prospect. She kept swaying, and Lucas had to keep his arm around her the whole time.

Not that she minded.

She liked his arm around her.

When they made it up the stairs and into their apartment, she gave a little cheer in victory. Then she remembered Michelle and Steve might be there, so she gave the victory cheer in a whisper instead.

Lucas was standing there smiling in a way she really liked.

She smiled back.

They stared at each other for what felt like a long time. Then Lucas gave himself a little shake and moved farther into the apartment.

"Michelle and Steve don't seem to be here," he said after looking around.

"That's okay then." She'd leaned over and was unzipping her boots, sighing in pleasure as she stepped out of them. "We can have some more fun."

"I don't know about fun. You probably want to go to bed," Lucas said.

She frowned at him. "Why would I go to bed?"

"Because you're just a little bit drunk."

"Oh." She blinked. Then nodded. Then blinked again. "I guess I am. You're very observ-observant, you know."

"That I am." He sounded like he was smiling, but she was blurry again and couldn't quite tell. She let him lead her into her bedroom, and the sight of her bed gave her an idea.

She turned toward him and wound her arms around his neck. "I think we should have a little fun," she said in what was supposed to be a conspiratorial whisper.

Lucas's body seemed to get very tense. She noticed it particularly.

"What do you say?" she asked him, rubbing her breasts against him. She liked how it felt. She liked how he felt. She liked everything about him.

He made a choked sound and took a step back. "I don't think we should be having that kind of fun right now."

"Why not?" She stuck out her lip to show him she wasn't happy about things.

"Because when you're thinking clearly, that isn't something you want."

She grabbed for him again, sliding her hand down his lovely firm chest to his lovely firm belly and then even lower.

Something else was very firm, and she really liked the feel of it.

Lucas grabbed her wrist and pulled her hand away from the front of his pants. "Damn, baby, you're going to kill me. You can't do that."

"But I want to—"

"You might want to now, but I don't think you want to for real. So we're not going to have that kind of fun tonight. Why don't you get in bed?" His voice sounded slightly rough, strained.

With a little whimper, she flopped down onto her bed fully dressed. "I don't have my pajamas on."

He went to her dresser and opened the top drawer where she kept her pajamas.

"I want the pink ones," she told him.

He found the pink ones and carried them over to her, and she pulled her little baby doll dress over her head and then got rid of her bra so she could put the pajamas on.

"Oh fuck," Lucas muttered, turning his back to her.

She blinked at him, wondering why he was all tense again. But she was too fuzzy to figure it out.

Her pajamas were fuzzy too, so they seemed to match her.

She got them on and stretched out on her bed. "I'm done," she told him so he could turn back around.

She stared up at him. The edges of his face and body faded into the dim light of the room. "I'm going to bed now."

"Good. That sounds like a good plan."

"Are you going to bed too?"

"Probably. I'll have to take a shower first."

"Oh." She couldn't figure that out, so she let it pass. "Thank you for tonight."

"You're welcome."

"You sure you don't want to come to bed with me?"

He made another one of those choked sounds. "I do, baby. Of course I do. But I can't tonight."

"Okay," she said with a sigh, closing her eyes and thinking sleep sounded pretty good. Almost as good as having fun with Lucas had sounded.

She thought she heard him leaving the room when she remembered something else. "Lucas?"

"Yeah?"

She opened her eyes and saw he had stopped just in front of her door. "What was your bam?"

He paused for a really long time. Then, "I'll tell you some other time."

"Okay."

Her head was spinning now, so she closed her eyes again.

She wanted to know what his bam was.

She wanted to know everything about him.
She wanted to go to bed with him.
She wanted a lot of things.
But right now she just wanted to go to sleep.
So she did.

Six

The next morning, Jill woke up feeling heavy and disoriented and headachy. Her mouth was dry, and her stomach was unsettled, and she could barely open her eyes.

When she managed to get up, go to the bathroom, and pull herself together, she started to remember some of last night. She'd gone to dinner with Lucas. They'd drunk a lot and eaten a lot and had a good time.

Then they'd started to walk home.

That much she remembered.

She couldn't recall much else, although she had vague images of Lucas in her bedroom. She had a sinking feeling she might have done something embarrassing, but she couldn't for the life of her remember what it was.

It was after ten when she made it out of her bedroom, but no one else was around. Steve and Michelle's bedroom door was open, but they weren't in the kitchen or living room. They must have gone somewhere—hopefully together if they'd managed to make up after the fight last night.

Lucas's bedroom door was closed. He was always up by now, but he wasn't in the living room or kitchen.

She made some coffee and drank it, trying to clear her mind and remember if she had anything to be embarrassed about. The evening's events were too fuzzy though. She couldn't dig deep enough to figure it out.

When she'd finished her coffee, she stood up, steeling her nerve.

She wasn't going to sit around and stew about how she might have humiliated herself. If she was going to find out, she would need to ask.

She just hoped it wasn't too bad.

She went back down the hall and knocked on Lucas's door.

He opened it almost immediately, and her eyes widened when she saw that his hair was wet and he was wearing nothing but a towel around his waist.

Her eyes might have slipped down to check out his body. How could she help it? His body was far too fine for her mental health.

"How are you feeling?" he asked, rubbing his wet hair with one hand. He didn't appear at all self-conscious about his lack of clothes.

"I'm fine. Headache but not too bad."

"Yeah. You had a lot to drink. I did too, if you want to know the truth." He gave her a little smile that made her nervousness ease a bit.

"I... I don't remember much about... about last night. After we left the restaurant, I mean."

"We didn't do anything," he said quickly.

"I know. I know. That's not what I meant. I was just wondering..." She cleared her throat. "Did I... did I do anything embarrassing? I feel like I might have."

His expression softened almost imperceptibly. "No."

She sucked in a breath. "That makes me think that I did."

"Why would you think you did when I just said that you didn't?"

"Because you sounded almost... gentle about it. Tell me the truth. What did I do?"

The corner of his mouth went up just slightly. "You were kind of out of it when we got home. You came on to me a little. No big deal."

She swallowed hard. She'd suspected she might have done something like that. "What did I do?"

"Jill, it really doesn't matter—"

"It matters to me!"

He let out a breath. "You felt me up a little. I knew you'd had too much to drink. Things like that happen. It's really no big deal."

She felt a serious mental cringe at the thought, but she made herself shake it off. He was right. Things like that happened.

Even to her occasionally.

"Sorry," she said.

He shook his head. "Nothing to be sorry about."

"Thanks for... for being a decent guy."

The other corner of his mouth went up too. "You're welcome."

They stared at each other for a minute.

"Oh," she said, remembering something else. "I did want to..."

When she trailed off, he prompted, "What?"

"I had a favor to ask of you, but I'm the one who should be doing you a favor after last night."

"Don't be ridiculous," he muttered, sounding impatient for the first time. "What's the favor?"

She was aware of a mental resistance but pushed through it since he seemed perfectly amenable to doing her a favor. "It's fine if you don't want to, but I have to go to a wedding next weekend. My boss's. I'm friends with her too, so I have to go. I mean, I want to go. But none of my friends are going. It's just people from work that I'd know there. And I'm not dating anyone now, and I don't really want to—"

"You want me to go with you?" he asked, breaking into her rambles. "That would be fine."

She let out a shuddering breath, almost giggling in her relief at getting the invitation said. She'd been mulling over it for weeks now, and she couldn't think of a better option than going to the wedding with him. "Just as friends, you know. You don't have to pretend to be my boyfriend. I just want someone to go with me."

"I get it. I don't mind going."

"Are you sure? I know weddings aren't that exciting, but I would really appreciate it."

"Sure," he said, adjusting the towel around his waist and bringing attention to his lean hips and flat abs. "It's in town, isn't it?"

"Oh, yeah. It's in town, and I don't think it's super formal or anything. And we don't have to stay at the reception very long."

"I don't mind weddings. Is there an open bar?"

"I think so."

"Then I'm definitely in." He gave her a grin that was almost rakish.

She giggled again. "Thanks."

"No problem."

"And thanks for... for last night."

"That was no problem either."

"Okay."

"Okay."

Her eyes slipped down again, so she made herself turn away at last, leaving him with his towel and his room.

~

A few evenings later, Jill and Michelle were hanging out in the living room together.

Jill was curled up in a corner of the couch, watching television and occasionally playing on her phone. Michelle was sitting on the floor, leaning back against the couch with her laptop propped on her thighs.

The guys had gone to work out at the gym. Or rather Lucas had gone to work out and Steve had gone to pretend to work out and to keep Lucas company.

Steve wasn't much into exercise.

Jill was enjoying the quiet, but she happened to glance down and see something unusual on the screen of Michelle's laptop. "What's that?"

Michelle glanced up to verify what Jill was asking, and then she raised her laptop so Jill could see better. "It's a budget. For me. Lucas helped me set it up."

"Seriously? Lucas did?"

"Yeah." Michelle's eyes were wide and her brows were lifted. "He went over everything with me, and we set up a budget so I can actually start saving a little money. Why are you so surprised? That's what he does for a living, you know."

"I know he does. I didn't mean..." Jill trailed off and then started again. "I know he's an accountant, but I didn't think he worked much anymore. I didn't realize he'd helped you with that."

"Well, he did. He did Steve's first, and I thought it was so cool that he said he would help me too. He's really good at it. I never would have thought it was possible for me to save any money, living on student loans and my assistantship. But we've got it worked out. It's not much, but it's something. Lucas is really... really pretty great."

Ridiculously, Jill was leaning into the words, wanting to hear them, wanting to hear about how great Lucas was— professionally as well as personally.

She wished he still wanted to work.

She wished he hadn't tossed all his ambition aside because of whatever had broken him two years ago.

She wished she knew what it was.

"You shouldn't be so surprised," Michelle said as if she were reading at least a few of her reflections. "Lucas isn't really the loser you think he is."

"I don't think he's a loser! I don't! You know I like him now."

"I know you do." Michelle's expression was earnest in that way she had, as if she were putting aside all teasing and laughter for the moment. "Y'all get along great. But you still... you still seem to think about him in only one way, as only this guy who hangs around and is kind of a slacker about everything. I know you like your life to always stay neat and orderly, and I can totally understand that, but people don't always fit into one little compartment and stay there."

"I know they don't." Jill was frowning, automatically defensive. "But Lucas is kind of a slacker. You know he is. He won't even work if he doesn't have to."

"I know. And I don't think it's good that he won't. But I do think it's his way of coping with something that happened to him."

"Do you know what it was?" Jill was torn between wanting to know and not wanting Lucas to have confided in Michelle and not in her.

"No. He won't ever talk about it. But something happened to him. It must have been something bad. He's been... trying to cope with it."

"I know he is."

"So if you know that, then you know that he won't necessarily always be like this. People heal. People learn to deal with what life does to them. People get better. Why shouldn't he get better too? Why can't he eventually change?"

Jill stared at her friend, stunned speechless by the idea.

Of course Lucas could change.

Of course Lucas could heal.

And it was wrong for her to keep him in that safe little box, assuming he'd always only be one way.

He wasn't just a slacker.

He was a person, just like her.

And he could change.

He could get better.

She gave Michelle a sheepish smile. "You're right. You're totally right."

"I didn't mean to give you a little lecture about it."

"Well, I deserved a little lecture. You're totally right. I know how great Lucas is. I really do. But I have been kind of... forcing him into a box. It just felt... safer that way."

"Yeah," Michelle murmured. "I kind of had a feeling about that."

Jill felt herself blushing slightly, but she didn't deny the implication. She didn't like to keep secrets from Michelle, and her feelings about Lucas definitely weren't easy or safe.

With a sigh, she said, "Just think how much I've changed since I moved here. When you first met me, did you ever think I'd be anything except that silly, clinging girl who followed a man around and tried to mold herself into what he wanted because she was too scared to let him go?"

"You weren't that bad," Michelle said, immediately defending Jill, even against Jill herself. "You were never that bad. You just... wanted a stable life, and you thought you'd found it in Ted. It was totally understandable."

"Maybe. But I'm glad I changed. I'm glad I... got better. I'm a lot happier not pouring myself out to keep a man who would only give me a few pieces of himself."

"Well, yeah. Obviously. We're all a lot happier when we're not doing that."

~

Lucas didn't mind weddings.

And he didn't mind helping Jill out by attending this one with her even though she'd made it very clear it wasn't a date.

He liked being Jill's friend, and he liked helping her out. Going to a wedding for a couple of hours wasn't any sort of burden, particularly since his schedule was loose most of the time.

But Jill could have worn a different dress.

She definitely should have worn a different dress.

A dress that looked less like lingerie.

He would have been much happier and more comfortable if she had.

It wasn't that her dress exposed an inappropriate amount of skin. It was short, but women's dresses were often short and there was nothing wrong with that. It was made like a sundress.

A lot of women had sundresses on at the wedding today even though it was a little chilly.

Jill had been wearing some sort of little sweater when they'd left.

He'd thought she'd looked pretty and had been perfectly comfortable with the whole situation.

Then she'd taken her sweater off when they got settled in their pew in the church.

Her dress had thick lace straps and some sort of a thin sash just under her breasts. It was made of a thin material—not silk or satin but something that looked like it was slippery—and it was a pale purplish-pink color.

It could have been lingerie, one of those little gown things women wore when they wanted to look sexy. That's what it made Lucas think of anyway.

And now he couldn't think of anything else.

He was trying to be a decent guy. He was going out of his way to not make a move on Jill, no matter how much he wanted to. He'd resisted even when she'd had her hands all over him and was tempting him into bed with her.

He was trying to be good, and the universe was conspiring to torture him for it.

Jill was sitting beside him wearing lingerie, and he couldn't drag his eyes away from her.

She wasn't showing any cleavage at all, but the fabric seemed to cling to the curve of her breasts. They looked touchable.

So touchable.

Nothing but touchable.

And he wasn't allowed to touch.

His body definitely wasn't remembering that fact.

He was uncomfortably aroused as the wedding progressed, and it wasn't going away. Instead of watching the bride and groom, his eyes kept slipping over to Jill beside him.

Her legs were crossed, and she seemed to have some sort of stockings on. Not thick tights like she often wore. Something thin with lace on the top. He knew that because once her skirt had slipped a little too high, and he had immediately taken notice.

The church was full. The couple was obviously popular, and it felt like half the town was in attendance. So he had to sit very close to Jill because there were so many people squeezed into the pew. He'd draped an arm around the back of the seat to get it out of the way, but it ended up around her.

He could smell her.

He could feel every time she made the smallest movement.

And she might as well have been wearing lingerie.

He shifted in his seat again, praying that the wedding would be over soon.

The bride and groom were exchanging vows. They both looked incredibly happy.

Lucas would have been happy for them had he not been suffering torture at the moment.

Why the hell had Jill worn that dress?

When the ceremony finally wrapped up and the wedding party recessed out, Lucas almost groaned in relief.

He needed to stand up.

He needed some air.

He needed to get away from Jill for a few minutes so he could get his body back under control.

When everyone stood up and started filing out of their pews, Lucas stretched his back and buttoned his suit jacket quickly, hoping it would hide his physical condition from any stray looks. When he saw Jill's little sweater lying on the pew, he picked it up and draped it over one wrist, using it to better shield the part in question.

She glanced back at him. "I was going to get that."

"No problem." It sounded like he was grumbling because his voice was too thick, but there wasn't anything he could do about that.

Jill shot him a quick look as they waited for their pew to start moving out into the main aisle. "You didn't have to come if you were going to be in a bad mood about it."

"What?" Lucas asked with a flash of annoyance because Jill was obviously so clueless about all the ways he was suffering.

"You didn't have to come."

"I wanted to come. I'm not in a bad mood."

"You could have fooled me. All that fidgeting through the whole service, and now all the grumbling."

"I'm not grumbling." He objected on principle even though he himself had realized it sounded like he was grumbling just a minute before.

She gave him an impatient look but didn't argue. She was starting to walk, and he followed her, but evidently she'd started too soon.

She had to come to an abrupt halt when the person in front of her stopped, and Lucas was in the middle of taking a step so he ran right into her.

The impact jarred his body quiet dangerously.

He smothered a groan as his arousal throbbed intensely. He needed to step backward. He was pressed up against her back. But her little body was warm and soft and everything he wanted.

He didn't pull back quite quickly enough.

Jill sucked in a quick breath and whirled around, her eyes wide. "What?" she gasped. "What?"

"What what?" he asked, although he knew exactly what she was responding to.

She'd evidently felt his condition.

It was kind of hard to miss at the moment.

She was looking down to where he was draping the sweater, and her expression was confused and strangely urgent. "What the hell, Lucas?"

There wasn't anything he could say.

He was turned on. Shamelessly turned on.

In the middle of church at an afternoon wedding.

Jill was looking around now, that same urgency on her face. "What's gotten into you? Were you sitting there leering at someone during the wedding? What's wrong with you?" She was talking softly. Almost a whisper.

Lucas replied in the same hushed tone, even though his words were indignant. She evidently had no idea that he'd gotten turned on by her. She was looking around for someone else who might have done that to him. "What's wrong with me? With *me*? You're the one wearing that dress."

The people in their pew had moved on, but Jill was clearly too distracted to take her turn. She looked down at herself in obvious bewilderment and then glared up at him. "What's wrong with my dress?"

"It's... it's..."

"It's what?" She examined herself again and then turned her head to scan the rows of people leaving the church, as if comparing her outfit to other women's to verify its appropriateness.

"It's like underwear!" Lucas burst out in that same harsh whisper.

She gasped again and crossed her arms over her chest in what was almost certainly an instinctive gesture. "It is not. It doesn't show that much skin. It doesn't!"

"I don't care how much skin it shows. It makes me think about underwear, and I'm sorry, but my body responds to that."

"You're crazy! It's not like underwear. It's a normal dress." She appeared torn between annoyance and self-consciousness and confusion, and it wasn't at all clear which one would come out on top. "Look at her dress over there, and then tell me something's wrong with mine."

Lucas looked over, scanning the young woman in question. Her dress was made almost exactly like Jill's—just a different color and with thinner straps. He could see that objectively.

But the other woman's dress didn't fire up all the lust in his body. It didn't get him all wound up this way.

Jill's did.

So he knew there was a difference.

"I'm not showing cleavage or anything," Jill said. "There's nothing inappropriate about what I'm wearing."

He looked down toward her neckline and saw something else. "Look," he said, his muscles tightening again and his erection giving another throb at the outline of her tight nipples beneath the fabric of her dress.

She made a little choking sound when she saw what he was staring at. "I can't help that! And they weren't like that the whole time. It just happened, and it's your fault they did that!"

"Why is it my fault?"

"Because you're standing there all hot and sexy and turned on, and it's making my nipples... do things. I can't control them. It's not the dress. This is your fault!" She was still talking as soft as ever, but she might as well have been yelling at him. Her eyes were angry, and her hands were clenched at her sides.

Despite his physical condition, Lucas got one of those sudden flashes—a vision of them and their conversation from the outside—and it made his mouth twitch slightly.

She narrowed her eyes. "Don't you dare, Lucas. Don't you dare make me laugh. I'm angry with you right now, and you deserve it."

"I know I do," he said, his voice wobbling as much as his mouth.

Jill's response spilled over in a little giggle, and it was absolutely irresistible. He had to twist his hands in her sweater to stop himself from reaching out for her.

"Damn it, Lucas," she said, trying to hide her laughter with one hand. "This is all your fault."

"You're right," he admitted, smiling for real although his arousal was still painfully tight. "Making you laugh is my fault. And your nipples are my fault. And getting turned on is my fault too. It's not the fault of your lingerie dress."

"It's not lingerie. It's a perfectly good dress." She looked around her and then said in a stage whisper, "But give me back my sweater. I'm going to put it on."

"No way. I need your sweater at the moment. It's serving a strategic purpose."

"I need it! I've got to go to the reception at my boss's wedding, and I don't want anyone else to mistake my dress for underwear." When Lucas didn't move, she added, "Take off your jacket and use that. I need my sweater."

That seemed like a reasonable compromise, so he handed the sweater back and replaced it with his suit jacket.

Even when she put the sweater on, Lucas's body didn't really behave itself.

He wanted her as much now as he had before.

It had been more than six weeks since they'd had their night together. His desire should be diminishing by now. He should be ready to move on.

He always was.

He rode the tide, waiting for it take him wherever it wanted to go.

He was normally ready for it by now.

But he wasn't.

He still wanted her just as much, and it didn't seem to matter what she was wearing.

He wanted her just the same.

Despite the fiasco over her dress, Jill had a really good time at the reception. Lucas found a restroom and came back in much better condition.

And she had fun with him.

She enjoyed him.

The reception was just heavy hors d'oeuvres, so they didn't have to sit through a long, plated dinner. They found a well-positioned table and stuffed themselves on yummy food and champagne. Lucas was engaging and amusing, and he charmed everyone who came over to say hello to her. And he even danced with her after the bride and groom had had their first dance.

He wasn't much of a dancer, and she wasn't either, but it didn't matter. They moved together, and she enjoyed it, and as far as she could tell he did too.

She'd been planning to stay at the reception an hour at the longest, but two hours passed and she had no pressing desire to leave.

She did have to eventually go the bathroom, and as she was coming out, she ran into Carol, the bride.

"Jill!" Carol said, reaching out to give her a hug. "Thank you so much for coming!"

"Thank you for inviting me. It was beautiful. I'm so happy for you and Patrick."

"I'm so happy for us too," Carol said, flushed and visibly emotional. "I can't believe we're actually married. I've been crazy about him for what feels like forever."

"Well, no one deserves to be happy more than you do." Jill meant what she said. Carol was one of the most genuinely good-hearted people she had ever met.

"Now tell me about your date," Carol said in a different tone. "He's absolutely gorgeous!"

Jill felt herself blushing. "Oh. He's... he's not really my date."

"He's sure acting like your date. I see the way he's been looking at you."

"Oh no. No. It's nothing like that. He's actually my roommate. He's the guy who moved into our spare room. Remember? I was wanting you to move in?"

"Yes, I remember. You didn't want to move in with another guy. But what a guy he turned out to be."

Jill shook her head. She felt fluttery, but she knew that was dangerous, so she tried to stamp the flutters out. "It's really not like that. I mean, I like him. A lot. And he's obviously... I mean, he looks the way he looks. But it would never work between us. We want totally different things. He's... he's not looking for a real relationship, and you know that's what I want."

Carol's face fell slightly. "Oh. That's really a shame. He seems so... good for you. But there's no use in hoping for someone who wants something different from you."

"Yeah," Jill said, feeling kind of depressed even though she'd always known that was true.

Carol's mouth turned up slightly. "But at least you can have fun with him for a little while. Right? It doesn't mean you're giving up on what you want. It just means you haven't found it yet."

Jill stared at the other woman, feeling like she'd been hit with an emotional sledgehammer.

Why did she always have to compare Lucas to the mental image she'd constructed of her forever man? Why did she always have to judge him on those qualities?

Why couldn't she just take him for who he was? Why couldn't she just have a little fun with him?

She'd had one really good night with him.

Why shouldn't she have another?

She wanted to so much.

She wanted *him* so much.

"What is it?" Carol asked with a frown.

"Nothing." Jill shook herself off. "Nothing. You're absolutely right. At least I can have fun with him for a little while."

"Good for you." After giving her a little hug, Carol moved on, and Jill returned to the reception hall to find Lucas.

Lucas was incredible.

There was no denying that fact.

And he was only going to be around for a little while.

He wasn't her forever man, but why shouldn't she have a little fun with him while she could.

It didn't mean she was giving up on her forever.

It just meant she hadn't found him yet.

Lucas was leaning back in a chair, finishing off a glass of champagne. When she reached him, she tugged on his arm. "Dance with me again."

"Okay." He swallowed down the last of his glass, put it down, and put his hand on her back as they went back to the dance floor.

She wrapped her arms around him and pressed her body against him.

He adjusted his stance, easing back from her slightly.

She moved closer.

Lucas leaned down and said into her ear, "Uh, Jill? Remember what you were saying about your nipples being out of your control? There are parts of my body that are equally out of my control, and you're getting them going right now."

She was excited now. Her heart was doing a wild gallop. "I've got my sweater on over my dress."

His thick voice wafted against her ear. "It was never about the dress."

Her whole body leaped in excitement, and she pulled back enough to look him in the eyes.

"What's going on, Jill?" Lucas asked, sounding hoarse, slightly confused, careful.

"I still want what I want," she began.

"I know you do."

"And I know you're never going to want what I want. But..."

His eyebrows shot up. "But what?"

"But I'm wondering if maybe we can... we can just have a little fun. Until it's time for us both to move on."

He stared at her speechlessly, but a fire had awoken in the green of his eyes. It took her breath away.

"You're serious?" he asked at last.

"Yeah. I don't know why... why can't I just have a little fun? What would be wrong with that?"

"Nothing," he said thickly. "Nothing in the world would be wrong with that."

Then he kissed her. Right there on the dance floor. And after a minute her head was spinning, and she had to pull away because otherwise she would be doing some things to him that would be very inappropriate to do in public, particularly at her boss's wedding.

"Do you think we can go... go somewhere?" she asked, breathing raggedly. "To have fun."

"Definitely. Let's go now."

He put his hand on her back again and walked her out of the room and into the hallway.

"It's a long way to get home," she said, thinking about the endless distance between them and a convenient bed. Now that she'd decided she could have him again, she wanted him right now.

Right. Now.

"Is there a hotel close by?" he asked.

She thought. "Not really."

He muttered under his breath as they walked toward the back exit of the building to avoid the crowds lingering around the front.

"There's always the car," she said, not even embarrassed at the suggestion.

Lucas pushed in a partly opened door off the hallway and looked inside. "What about in here?"

She gave a little inhale and peered inside. It appeared to be some sort of dressing room, but it must not have been used for the wedding party because it was completely empty. There was a big mirror and an upholstered bench and a vanity and a rack for hanging clothes.

No one's stuff was in it. It didn't appear to be being used. No one was hanging out in this back hallway.

No one was even in sight.

And it was an empty room when they needed it.

She hesitated.

"There's a lock on the door," Lucas said, checking the doorknob.

"Good enough." She pushed the door closed, fumbling to lock it, and then she hauled him down into a kiss.

The kiss was deep and passionate immediately, as if weeks of longing had been all bottled up and suddenly channeled into the touch of their lips. Lucas stepped her back against one of the walls in the room, and he devoured her mouth, his body hard and hot and deliciously masculine. Trapping her in place.

She clawed at the back of his shirt, trying to get him even closer, and her tongue dueled and danced with his until it triggered shivers of pleasure all centered between her legs.

"Maybe we should move to the bench," she mumbled against his lips. His hands had been on her thighs, and now they were sliding up under her skirt, cupping her bottom in a deliciously possessive way.

"Why?" His mouth was moving down her neck, sucking on little spots that made her jolt with pleasure.

"Because if I don't come pretty soon, I'm going to shatter into pieces. So I want to get past the standing-up part."

She meant it. It might have all happened in a hot, intense rush, but her body was trembling, tense, poised for a climax she desperately needed.

He chuckled. "I think I could make you come while you're standing."

"Ha." That was about as articulate a retort as she was capable of at the moment. Once his hands had found her breasts, she was arching into his palm, trying to get more friction where she needed it.

He was chuckling as he bent over far enough to nip at her breast through the fabric of her dress.

She cried out at the sharp surge of pleasure.

Then he was moving even lower, kneeling onto the floor.

"What are you doing?" she asked, breathless and slightly dazed.

"Making you come," he said with an almost wicked smile. "Just make sure you keep standing up."

Her eyes widened as he slid his hands up her thighs, moving her skirt up as he did. Then he tucked his fingers around the sides of her panties and pulled them down her legs.

"Oh God," she breathed as he moved his head between her legs.

Was he actually doing this?

And was she going to have to try to keep standing up the whole time?

Her knees were already starting to buckle.

He widened her stance with his hands and then pulled her hips away from the wall to give him access. Then he gave her another devilish smile and advanced with a little lick with his tongue.

She cried out before she could stop herself.

He seemed to like her reaction, and he chuckled again. Then he went to work with his fingers, mouth, and tongue. She couldn't really see what he was doing, but it felt incredible, and soon she was having to fight to not grind herself against his face.

She clutched at his head and pressed her back into the wall and tried desperately to make her legs hold herself up. She couldn't stay quiet as he worked her over, but she was vaguely conscious that they were in a building with a lot of other people, so she finally had to stuff her fist into her mouth to smother her sounds of pleasure.

He had two of his fingers inside her, and he was sucking hard on her clit when she came undone completely. She sobbed around her fist, her body shaking helplessly as the orgasm ripped through her. She was still shuddering with little aftershocks when Lucas finally pulled his head away, grinning up at her with that smoldering amusement. The bottom half of his face was wet, and she wasn't even embarrassed.

"And you stayed on your feet the whole time," he said.

She half giggled and half sobbed as she pulled him up so she could hug him. He held her against him for a minute, his embrace tense, tight, almost needy.

But he was rocking into her slightly, and she knew he was really turned on. He'd taken the time to give her pleasure, no matter how urgent his own arousal was, and she didn't fail to recognize that.

Plus she hadn't had nearly enough.

"Now should we use the bench?" she asked against his shoulder. "Or did you want to do the next part standing up too?"

He choked on a laugh and then kissed her again, hefting her up as he did. She wrapped her legs around him, and he carried her over to the bench, easing her down on her back and moving on top of her.

"Please tell me you have a condom," she mumbled against his mouth.

"I always have a condom."

"Good man."

Her legs were still wrapped around him, and she was grinding against the bulge of his erection. He was grinding back.

He pulled away long enough to dig the condom out of his wallet, and she worked on his trousers as he unwrapped it. They didn't even take off his pants or underwear—just pushed them down enough to be out of the way. Then he put the condom on and positioned himself between her legs.

Then he was finally, finally easing inside her.

"Oh God!" She gasped, arching her neck in pleasure at the tight penetration. She hadn't had sex since she'd had sex with Lucas six weeks ago, and it felt like forever.

She needed this.

She needed it bad.

"Oh fuck, that's right, that's so good, you feel so good." Lucas was muttering out the words as he rolled his hips slightly, moving himself just slightly inside her.

"Lucas, please," she breathed. She pumped her hips from below. "I need... I need... oh please."

With a low groan, he started to thrust, building up a fast, steady rhythm that matched the pumps of her hips.

She was whimpering with how good it felt, how the motion seemed to come from her deepest core, how it triggered nerve endings all over her body. She slid her hands down to his ass, feeling the firm muscles as he worked his hips.

This was what she wanted.

This was so much what she wanted.

And she didn't want it to end.

He fucked her like that until she came, choking on her release. Then without a word, he pulled out, turned her over the bench, and entered her from behind.

Then he got going again, and she was shocked to feel her body responding.

Again.

It couldn't seem to get enough of him.

She was making the most embarrassing sounds—somewhere between grunts and sobs, as he pumped into her, his body pressed into her back, his skin making a slapping sound as it hit her bottom.

"Lucas," she heard herself gasping. "Lucas. Lucas. Oh God. Lucas." She was trying to cling to the bench, but she kept turning her head to look at him behind her.

She liked the tension of his face, the heat in his eyes, the sheen of sweat on his skin. She liked how he was totally into this.

Just as much as she was.

He reached around her body until he was pressing his fingertips against her clit. He wasn't really rubbing it. Just pressing against it. And it was exactly what she needed.

She bit her lip to smother a loud cry of pleasure.

"Oh fuck, baby," Lucas was saying, as if the words were dragged out of him. He slowed down his thrusting momentarily and panted against her neck. He rolled his hips and pressed her clit, and she squeezed all around him, helplessly responding to him. "That's right. That's so good. I love your little body. I love it so much. So hot and tight. So responsive to me. I love how you feel."

He rolled his hips again, and she came hard, gasping against the upholstery of the bench.

"So good," he was muttering. "You're so good for me, baby. So good."

He braced himself with his free hand and started to pump hard.

"Yeah!" she breathed. "Hard. As hard as you want. Lucas, please. I want you… I want you…" She couldn't finish a complete sentence, but she didn't need to.

Lucas had finally let himself go, and she turned her head to watch the pleasure twisting on his face.

He let out a low roar as he fell over the edge, his body jerking behind her.

He was still groaning softly as his body started to relax. His ragged breath was blowing her hair just a little.

Jill was blazing hot and exhausted and slightly uncomfortable from their position, and she was so wet that it was trickling down the inside of her thighs.

She couldn't remember ever having sex like this before.

She couldn't remember ever being so physically sated, like her body had nothing more to need at the moment, like it had been given everything it could ever want.

"Oh God," she kept saying, unable to stop.

Lucas just made wordless grunts, but he finally found the energy to pull out of her and take care of the condom.

With him having moved, she could readjust her body onto her back and collapse on the bench, gasping loudly and wiping sweat off her face.

There wasn't room on the bench for Lucas, so he collapsed on the floor, his back against the wall.

They looked at each other, smiling and panting, for a long time.

Finally Lucas seemed to find his voice. "Well, you wanted to have a little fun. Would you call that fun?"

She gave a little giggle. "That was the most fun I can ever remember having."

"Me too."

She couldn't help but like the sound of that.

Seven

At four the following morning, Jill was having sex with Lucas again.

She hadn't planned it. In fact, she wasn't sure how it had even happened. They'd gone home after the wedding, and Michelle and Steve were there and getting along again, so the four of them had spent a friendly evening of pizza and Netflix together.

Occasionally she'd glance over at Lucas and find him looking at her, but they hadn't said a word about having sex, and then they'd all gone to bed.

Jill had woken up at 3:57 a.m. Wide awake. Her mind whirling with what had happened with Lucas at the wedding and her body still feeling him inside her. She'd had to get up out of bed to distract herself, going to the bathroom and then to the kitchen for a cold bottle of water.

On her way back to her room, Lucas's door had opened. She stopped, startled and disoriented. He stood in his doorway, wearing nothing but a pair of boxer briefs, his hair practically standing up on end like he'd gone to sleep with it damp.

They didn't say a word.

He just pulled her into his room, closing the door behind them. Then she was in the small bed with him, and his body was moving over her, his mouth on her lips, her throat, her cheekbone. He yanked up her pajama top so he could reach her breasts, and her fingers were tucked into the sides of his underwear, holding on. Just holding on.

The world was a hot, dark haze of pleasure, and she had no idea how long it was until Lucas was fumbling with a condom and then pushing himself inside her.

She wrapped her legs fully around his waist, hooking her ankles so they'd stay, as he rocked into her. He was slow and steady and so exactly right as he levered his hips with each thrust. It felt like he was watching her, even in the dark. It felt like he knew everything she was thinking, everything she was feeling.

She made sure to stay quiet as the pleasure overwhelmed her, turning her head to stifle the sounds she was making into a pillow. Lucas was grunting steadily, but they were soft and hoarse. Sometimes he said her name. Sometimes he said how good she felt. Sometimes he said how much he wanted, needed this. The cheap twin bedframe was squeaking but not too loudly or gratingly. All of it washed over her, mingling with the sensations, pushing her over the edge.

He only fell out of rhythm at the very end, his hips jerking against hers as she squeezed hard around him. Then he fell down on top of her and she clung to him like a lifeline.

They couldn't stay like that for very long. The condom always got in the way. So soon Lucas was getting up, going to the door of the room, glancing out in the hall as if to make sure no one else was up, and then walking across to the hall bathroom to take care of the condom and clean up.

Jill stayed where she was. She was hot and relaxed and didn't want to move yet. It wasn't even five yet, and Michelle and Steve never got up early on Sunday mornings.

When Lucas returned, he switched on a light on the small dresser so the room wasn't quite so dark. He came over and dropped into the bed beside her. There was room for both of them side by side, but just barely. She was under the sheet, but he didn't try to cover up. He stretched his big body and then turned his head in her direction and smiled.

"Now that's the way to start the week," he said, his voice warm, relaxed, leisurely.

For no good reason, the comment made her heart drop stupidly.

There was nothing wrong with what he'd said. It wasn't crude or insensitive or selfish. In fact, he was clearly giving her a compliment and letting her know how much he'd enjoyed having sex with her.

But it so perfectly highlighted the truth about what sex with her meant to him.

A good time.

Nothing but a good time.

And she knew it. Of course she knew it. She'd gone into this with her eyes wide open. She'd made a conscious decision to have a good time with him for a little while before she started to look again for her forever man.

This was what she'd wanted.

And it was exactly what he was giving her.

But she suddenly knew—knew so deeply that it made her body stiffen—that she had to be very careful here. If she didn't guard herself carefully, she was going to be wanting more from Lucas than he was capable of giving her.

Yes, he could change. He was capable of change.

But she couldn't count on him to change.

He'd told her he didn't want any long-term commitments. He'd told her he always moved on. And she had to believe him.

She couldn't hope for more from this.

She would get her heart broken. Broken so badly it would take ages to recover.

Lucas was never going to be her boyfriend—much less her forever man—so she could never let herself start thinking about him that way.

"You okay?" he asked, his tone different now.

"Y-yeah."

"Is that a real yeah?"

She smiled, sorting through her feelings at last. "Yeah, it's a real yeah. Sorry. Just recovering from all that great sex we just had."

He smiled back, but his eyes were watchful. She wasn't sure if he believed her or not.

She sat up, suddenly feeling exposed despite the fact that she was covered up with the sheet. "Do you know what happened to my top?"

They both looked around the bed, and then Lucas rolled over onto his side and reached down to the floor to snag her pajama top.

As she put it on, she couldn't help but notice the long, ragged scar down the side of his back, leading down beneath the waistband of his underwear.

Unable to stop herself, she reached over and traced the line of it with her fingertips.

She felt him freeze for a moment with a tension deeper than physical.

She didn't say anything as she touched his scar. She wondered what had happened to him, what had hurt him so badly.

What wound was taking so long to heal inside him.

His body was so strong, so lean and hard and powerful.

Something had ripped it apart.

Something had hurt him very badly.

She couldn't stand the thought of it.

Finally he rolled onto his back, hiding the scar from her. He gave her a wary look and didn't say anything.

He wasn't going to tell her.

A few stray memories had returned from that evening she'd gotten drunk with him, and she remembered him telling her that one day he would tell her about his bam. She wasn't sure why that moment had stuck with her despite the fuzziness of the rest of it, but it had.

He hadn't meant it though.

They were friends now. They were roommates. They'd had sex twice in the past twelve hours. And he still wasn't going to tell her.

He wasn't her boyfriend.

He didn't want to be her boyfriend.

And he never would.

When she met his eyes again, she could see he was waiting warily for her to ask about his scar again. She could see it on his face. He expected her to ask, and he was getting ready a rejection.

She didn't want to be rejected by him. It would hurt her feelings quite badly. She licked her lips and held the question back.

After a minute or two, she saw him relax.

She needed to say something eventually, so she finally said, "I don't really want Michelle and Steve to know about this."

"Yeah. I figured. No problem on my part."

She let out a sigh. "I don't think we should do this too often."

His body tightened again, just slightly. "Why not?"

"Because... because we haven't really gotten past where we were at the beginning. We want different things. And sex with you is... is really fun. But if we do it too often, I'm not going to be able to keep it casual."

It was kind of embarrassing to admit that, but she lived with Lucas, and honesty was the only way she knew how to deal with relationships.

His lips parted just slightly. "Ah."

"Yes. Having sex with a guy all the time is going to make me think relationship. And I know you don't want that."

So the truth she discovered was that she was still a little silly. She realized it then. Because part of her was holding its breath, waiting to hear his response. Hoping just a tiny bit for a denial, for him to change his mind.

For him to tell her that he might want more than sex from her.

There was a pause that fed her hopes, but then he said, "Yeah. That makes sense. No sense in confusing matters."

So there it was.

Just sex.

No relationship.

He didn't want commitments.

He didn't want normal life responsibilities.

He didn't want obligations that would make him do something—anything—he didn't want to do.

He wanted to ride the tide. He wanted to only go where it took him.

He wasn't ever going to work to get somewhere else.

"I do like the idea of occasionally having fun with you like this," she said, pleased her voice was controlled, natural. "But I think we better not make it too often."

"So... how often?" He slanted her a questioning look. If she didn't know better, she would have said it was urgent, as if her answer really mattered to him.

"I don't know," she admitted. "I'll have to kind of... feel it out. Maybe we should just say we can have sex if it feels right and we both want to and neither of us has anyone... anyone else."

"I'm not going to have anyone else," he said softly. "And I'm always going to want to have sex with you. No matter what. So just let me know if it feels right to you. Any time."

She swallowed hard. He was leaving it all to her. Which made sense. He could do sex casually. She couldn't. Not much anyway. And not for long.

"Okay," she said with a smile that didn't waver. "Sounds like a plan."

She wondered how long it would be before she felt like having sex with Lucas again would be safe.

He'd told her they could have sex any time she wanted.

At the moment, she really had no idea how long she would last.

~

Two months later, Lucas was wondering when Jill would ask him to have sex again.

Since their weekend at the wedding, they'd only had sex once—four and a half weeks ago. He still didn't know what had prompted it, but she'd knocked on his door at about two o'clock in the morning one night and had gotten half a stilted question out before he'd dragged her into his room, into his bed.

They'd had sex over and over again that night. He'd known she was likely to withdraw when the sun came up, so he'd made it last as long as his body could handle.

The memory of that night—of all three nights he'd spent in bed with Jill—still came to him far too often, making him sweat, making him pant, making him hard.

He understood why she was being careful, but she wasn't dating anyone else. She didn't really seem to be trying to find a relationship as far as he could tell since she hadn't had a date in the past two months. He didn't understand why they couldn't keep having sex.

It wouldn't be the end of the world if she treated him like a boyfriend. He liked hanging out with her. He liked talking to her. He liked doing things with her. He liked having sex with her.

They were two reasonable adults, and they could handle any awkward consequences that might come up.

He didn't like the distance he could feel between him and her.

And his body really didn't like being deprived this way, especially when it saw Jill every single day, little and clever and gorgeous and soft and absolutely irresistible.

Occasionally he even thought about moving out of the apartment even though he had more than two months left in his lease. It would be easier if he didn't see Jill at all. Maybe then he could finally get her out of his mind, out of his life.

But he never did.

He really liked it in Blacksburg, in this apartment, with Jill.

He didn't want to move yet.

He just wanted to have sex with her again.

He wanted to have sex. Full stop. And he hadn't. At all. Not with anyone other than Jill.

Not since his first time with her.

He had no idea why.

It was annoying.

Sex just wasn't serious to him, and since he never made any promises to women, he was never in the position to take advantage of them or betray their trust. He could have sex with anyone he wanted.

But he couldn't.

At least he hadn't.

Not in ages.

More than once, he'd gone out in the evenings, determined to find a woman to sleep with. His body needed the release, and he was hoping being with someone different would finally break these strange invisible bonds Jill had tied him up with.

He'd gone to a bar. He'd chatted up more than one woman.

And nothing.

He hadn't left with any of them. He hadn't been able to rouse even the slightest bit of interest for them. He probably could have forced himself to go through with it anyway. He assumed (hoped, prayed) he still would have been able to get it up. But he couldn't bring himself to use another human being that way—as a body, an object to be utilized in an attempt to work out his own issues.

He'd never had sex when both he and the women hadn't been equally into it, and he wasn't going to start now, just because he was in this weird emotional prison shaped and controlled by Jill.

Soon she would want to have sex with him again.

Surely she would.

Please God, he hoped she would.

No amount of jerking off in the shower could take care of the degree of lust for her he was suffering on a daily basis.

It was a Saturday evening, and he should probably have gone out to try to distract himself. But Steve had come home with some new party game that used video elements and cards, and he bullied everyone into playing it with him. Jill's friend Chloe had come over too—she was loud, dramatic, and always made everyone laugh—so there were five of them playing the game, drinking beer and eating snacks, and Lucas had a ridiculously good time.

He'd never thought he was a game player, but maybe he was.

They stayed hanging out until late, and Michelle and Jill walked Chloe out to her car after midnight, when she was finally ready to go home.

Lucas was on one of the couches, leaning back with a beer in his hand.

Steve was sitting beside him, and he was grinning as he said, "Admit it, man. You're gonna miss us when you leave."

He'd been having a good night, but for some reason the casual words hit him hard. Lucas felt a kick of pain in his chest.

When he didn't answer, Steve frowned. "What's the matter with you?"

"Nothing," Lucas said quickly. "Just drank too much." He'd had three beers, but that wasn't anywhere near enough to affect his ability to think or function.

It was something else that had hit him.

Something emotional.

He *was* going to miss them. Not just Jill—all of them.

He didn't want to leave when his six months were up.

He didn't want to leave at all.

He was on the verge of settling here, and he knew what would happen when he did that.

He would be invested.

He would be vulnerable.

He would get hurt.

"You must be getting old if a few beers put you in this kind of stupor."

Lucas didn't respond to that. He didn't know what to say.

Steve must have been thinking about their conversation because after a minute of silence he said slowly, "Why don't you stay?"

"What?"

"Why don't you stay? After your six months are up, I mean. I don't think Chloe is going to be able to move back in yet, so we'll have that empty room. Why don't you stay?"

"Eh."

"What does that mean? You like it here, don't you?"

"Sure."

"You've been having a good time with us. Don't try to convince me you're not."

"I am. I like you all."

"And you're into Jill, aren't you?"

Lucas straightened up with a jerk. "What?"

Steve gave him a little smirk. "You heard me. I'm not totally clueless, you know. You're into Jill. It's pretty obvious. I think she might have a thing for you too, so why don't you do something about it?"

Lucas had genuinely no idea that anyone other than Jill knew anything about what was going on between them. He'd never been obvious with his feelings—even before when he'd thought of himself as wanting what everyone else wanted—so he wasn't sure what to make of the fact that Steve had picked them up so easily.

"I don't do relationships," he said at last, when it was clear Steve was waiting for a response.

"I know that's what you've been saying, but I don't get why you have to stick with it. If you're into her, what's the harm in changing your mind?"

"Are you really going to give me advice about relationships, when you spend half your time fighting with your own girlfriend?" Lucas's voice was light, not bitter, but he used the words intentionally to redirect the focus of the conversation. Away from him.

Away from answers he didn't have, couldn't say.

"Stop changing the subject," Steve said, not taking offense the way he could have. "What's your problem with relationships? You've always been a decent guy and not some sort of player or user. Weren't you engaged for a while?"

"Yeah."

"Did she burn you real bad?"

"No."

Carly hadn't burned him at all. Their breakup had been mutual.

And a relief.

"Then what's your deal?"

Lucas let out a long breath, wishing he was capable of explaining in a way that other people could understand.

"Relationships make things serious," he said at last.

Steve frowned. "Yeah? So what?"

Lucas didn't answer.

"Relationships make what serious?" Steve asked after a minute.

Lucas tightened his lips. "Life."

The word lingered in the air for a long time. Lucas was uncomfortable, exposed in a strange way.

Finally Steve leaned forward, starting to get up. "Shit, man, I don't know. I guess I don't know anything about it. But that doesn't sound right. That doesn't sound right to me at all."

He stood up, clapped Lucas on the shoulder, and then started collecting the bottles of beer scattered around the room.

Lucas just sat there for a long time, nursing his last swallow of beer.

~

Later, Lucas came out of his room in his underwear, after having taken a shower before bed. Michelle and Steve's door was closed, so they'd obviously gone to bed already.

But Jill was still up, sweeping the floor in the living room where they'd gotten crumbs from their snacks.

He stood and watched her for a moment, the way she worked so busily, straightening cushions, making the room look neat and comfortable and inviting again.

Turning a shared apartment into a home.

She was wearing a pair of leggings and a long sweater, and she looked tiny, curvy, like Jill.

When she became aware of his presence, her eyes widened. "Hey. I didn't hear you come out."

"I was just getting some water. You don't have to do all that yourself, you know." He gestured toward the broom she still held.

"I know. I don't mind. I like for things to be nice when I wake up in the morning. I hate mess waiting for me when I get up."

"You want me to help?"

"Nah." She smiled at him, relaxed and friendly and like he was nothing in the world to her but her roommate. "There's nothing else to do."

"Okay."

She seemed to notice that he was just standing there because she came closer, pausing about a foot away from him. "Is everything all right?"

"Yeah. Sure."

Her brows lowered. She was looking at him the way Steve had earlier. "Are you sure? You look…"

"What?"

"I don't know. Like something has gotten under your skin."

She'd gotten under his skin, and he couldn't get her out.

But it was even more than that.

He couldn't fully process it himself, much less put it into words.

"You had a good time tonight, didn't you?" she asked after a minute. Her eyes were almost gentle.

"Yeah. I did."

"Me too." She paused for a beat, dropping her eyes and then raising them again. "I'm glad you moved in with us."

His heart made a crazy leap. It wasn't his body. It was his heart. "Thanks," he mumbled gruffly.

She moved even closer and reached her hand out toward him. For a moment he thought she was making a move, that he might get to take her to bed tonight. Again. At last.

But she reached around his side to that stupid scar on his back and traced the line of it with her fingertips.

The light touch triggered so many sensations in his body, so many emotions in his soul. He shuddered with it, wondering how he was even capable of feeling so much, so deeply.

This felt serious.

He was vulnerable. So incredibly vulnerable right now.

He wanted this moment to last.

"Lucas," she breathed, her fingers still caressing his scar. She couldn't see it since it was on his back, but she seemed to know exactly where it was.

"Yes," he managed to say in a rasp.

Her eyes were huge and deep and so tender. "Can you tell me what your bam was?"

His mouth opened. The words were in his throat. Everything in him wanted to tell her, wanted to share it, wanted her to carry some of what always weighed him down.

Wanted to explain why he'd put his life on hold two years ago and was afraid to start it up again.

But the words didn't come out.

Nothing came out but a strange choked sound.

She waited. A full minute she waited.

Then she dropped her hand. Dropped her eyes. "Okay," she murmured. "Good night, Lucas."

She was disappointed. He knew she was.

And he hated that fact.

But he hated the idea of telling her even more.

~

The next day, Lucas was looking at his email. For the first time in a long time, there was work involved in doing so.

He presently had five emails in his inbox from people wanting him to help them with their money.

Michelle and Steve had evidently told everyone they knew how much he'd helped them with their budgets. Now other people were wanting him to help them too.

Three of them were fairly simple, involving people with limited income and nothing complicated in terms of taxes. Like Michelle and Steve, it would be just a couple of hours of work. Lucas would have helped them simply as favors to his friends, but everyone had offered to pay him.

The other two had small businesses, so the work involved would be more involved.

And Lucas was actually considering agreeing.

For the first time in ages, the idea of working didn't feel like a tedious nightmare to him. He'd enjoyed helping Steve and Michelle. And these projects didn't sound painful. He could just go over to their places, sit at a table, and talk them through everything.

He was still doing fine with his savings. He could live for more than two years on what he had left. But he liked the idea of having something else to think about. He liked the idea of doing something productive.

It was a new thought. A strange thought.

But maybe it was a good thing.

Making up his mind, he answered all five emails, telling them he'd be happy to help them and saying he'd give them a discount on his rate since they were friends of Steve and Michelle.

He was just finishing the final email when Steve and Michelle came out of their bedroom and into the living room.

Michelle went to pick up her purse, and Steve said, "Hey, we're going out to get something to eat. You want to come too?"

Lucas hadn't thought about dinner yet, but he liked the idea of going out. So he said, "Yeah, sure. That would be great. Should we call Jill and tell her?" It was after five, so Jill should be on her way home from work soon.

"I already texted her," Michelle said. "She's walking back from work now and is going to meet us outside."

Pleased with this news, Lucas closed his laptop and found his shoes. He left the apartment and walked downstairs with Michelle and Steve. When they got outside, he saw Jill down the block.

She wore a skirt and a sweater vest with a white shirt beneath it. She was carrying the big leather bag she always took to work. She waved when she saw them, and Lucas's heart did a ridiculous little leap.

Damn.

Damn.

He was so excited to see her.

There was a lot of traffic in downtown Blacksburg at this time of day, and there was a steady stream of cars passing by him. Because he'd been distracted by Jill, he hadn't realized that he was standing on the edge of the sidewalk, not far from the curb.

He got a glimpse of a large SUV passing by him just then, and he flinched and turned to look at the quickly approaching vehicle.

His heart dropped immediately, and the blood drained from his face in a cold chill of terror he simply couldn't control. He took several steps away from the curb and forced himself to focus on Jill, who had almost reached them.

She was pretty and smiling and warmly clever. And Lucas was cold and trying to keep his hands from shaking.

Jill said hello to all of them, but her smile faded as she looked at Lucas. "What's the matter?"

"Nothing."

Her frown deepened, but to his relief, she didn't press the point. She asked, "So where are we going to eat?"

They had a brief discussion before they decided on a little Greek place a few blocks away. When they started to walk, Michelle and Steve took the lead, and Jill fell in step beside Lucas.

She took his arm and looked up at him. "What's the matter?"

"Nothing. I said that before."

"Yeah, but you weren't telling me the truth. You were fine, and then you weren't. What happened?"

He hated himself for still feeling this way, even two years later.

He hated himself for being weak.

And he hated himself for letting Jill see exactly how weak he was.

He didn't say anything.

Just like his family, Jill would believe that what had happened to him wasn't big enough to justify his response to it. She wouldn't understand why it had changed everything for him.

She would think he was foolish, and he didn't want her to think that.

He wanted her to think he was...

"Lucas," Jill murmured. "You're worrying me."

He took a deep breath and pulled himself together by nothing more than the force of his will. "Sorry. I'm really fine. It's just one of those things."

She was peering at him closely, and he smiled at her. He was starting to feel better.

This didn't happen to him much.

Only occasionally did he still feel the impact, feel the *bam*.

He didn't want it to be important to him anymore, so he didn't want to make it important to Jill.

Things were already feeling far too serious to him with her.

If he told her, he'd never be able to drag himself away when it was time to leave.

Eight

That weekend, late on Saturday morning, Jill was sitting at a table in a pretty corner of Tea for Two with Michelle and Chloe. Michelle had texted early that morning about another fight with Steve, so Chloe had called for an emergency summit over pastries.

They'd been hashing out Michelle's relationship for almost an hour now, and they'd all fallen into a silence that was heavy, reluctant.

No one wanted to say the next thing.

Finally Michelle, who'd been tearing up on and off for a while now, put down her teacup and said, "I'm not ready to break up with him yet."

"Well, then don't," Jill said quickly. "You love him. It makes sense to try to work through everything."

"We've been working through things for months now, and it's not getting better. It's just getting worse. But still..." Her brown eyes were big and so sad.

"What about counseling or something?" Chloe asked in a tone far more serious than her typical flippant insouciance. "Do you think that would be worth a try?"

"Maybe. I don't know. I don't know if he'd go for that. He..." Michelle bit her lower lip. "I don't know."

"Well, talk to him about it," Jill said, trying to sound encouraging although she'd seen the end coming for Michelle and Steve for a while now. She dreaded the breakup, but she was sure it was coming soon. "See what he says."

"I will." Michelle leaned back in her chair and fiddled with a napkin with both hands. "I really thought he was the real thing."

"Maybe he is. It isn't always easy. In fact, relationships are never easy. He might be the real thing." Jill felt terrible as she said the words because she cared about Steve so much. He was her friend, and it felt like she was talking behind his back.

But Michelle had been her friend first. Michelle would always be first to her.

"All right," Michelle said, her expression clearing into something approximating a smile. "We need to talk about something else now."

"Okay," Chloe said, leaning forward and slanting Jill a look that was almost mischievous. "I want to talk about Lucas."

Jill's stomach twisted sickeningly.

If Chloe was about to announce that she suddenly had the hots for Lucas, Jill might be sick.

She'd still never told her friends about having sex with Lucas. She wasn't even sure why. But Chloe didn't know about it, and Lucas was a very attractive man. Only a fool wouldn't be interested in him.

"What about him?" Jill asked carefully.

"Are you doing him or not?" Chloe asked as blandly as if she were asking about the traffic.

Jill froze. "What?"

"You heard me. Tell us the truth. I say you are, but Michelle said you couldn't be because you would have told us. So what is it for real?" Chloe's dark eyes were sparkling with interest.

Michelle was smiling now too, obviously relieved to think about something other than her own relationship. "We know something's going on, so don't even bother to deny it. We're just not sure exactly what."

Jill broke out of her frozen stance at last and kind of slumped forward against the table, almost taking down her empty teacup in the process. "Oh shit."

"Ha!" Chloe exclaimed. "I'm vindicated. You *are* doing him, aren't you?"

"I'm not doing him," Jill insisted in a harsh whisper, glancing around the shop. It was fairly busy at the moment, but there wasn't anyone she recognized except Emma, who ran the office she worked for, and Emma's handsome husband, who were sitting together in a far corner. Carol was working in the kitchen, and Ginny, who co-owned Tea for Two, was working the counter. No one was listening to what Jill was saying right now.

"You're not?" Michelle asked.

"Well..." Jill cleared her throat. "I have done him. A couple of times. But it's not currently happening."

Chloe gave a little squeal, and Michelle leaned forward to demand, "Tell us everything. Tell us right now."

So Jill finally told them. Everything. About meeting Lucas in the bar that night. About going back to his hotel room. About him showing up the next morning as her new roommate. About having sex with him again at the wedding. And then again. And then again. About how she wasn't going to sleep with him anymore—no matter how much she wanted to.

"Why didn't you tell us?" Chloe asked. "You've been going through all this on your own."

"I know. I know. I don't know why. I should have." Jill rubbed at her face, feeling guilty and confused. "I was just... just embarrassed, I guess."

"Embarrassed about what?"

"That I know he's not for me. I *know* it. And I… still can't seem to resist him."

"No one in the world could blame you for not being able to resist that man. I mean his shoulders alone." Chloe gave an exaggerated shiver. "There's nothing to be embarrassed about."

"And how do you know he's not for you? I've always thought he seemed pretty crazy about you," Michelle added.

"Really?" Jill's voice squeaked slightly, and she hated herself for it.

"Yes, really. But I thought maybe you'd told him it could never happen. I mean, he's not really your type. He doesn't have a job or anything. He doesn't have his life together. I thought maybe he was into you, you told him no, and he just hadn't gotten over it. I didn't know you actually like him."

Jill sighed. "I do. He's… pretty amazing. You're right about him not having his life together, but I've been trying not to be so rigid about that kind of thing. Like we were talking about before. It's really more than that. He doesn't want a serious relationship. He's actively against them. He'll never be able to make me happy and give me what I want. And yet I can't seem to… to move on, get over him. It's… embarrassing."

"It's normal," Chloe said firmly. "You can't always tell your heart how to feel."

"But you can tell your will to make choices you know are right." Jill was utterly serious about this, and her tone reflected it. "I can't try to convince myself he might change later on, so I should just take the little pieces he's willing to give me right now."

"No," Michelle said. "You'd end up getting really hurt."

"I know. I know. It's already hard enough. Can you imagine how I'd feel if I hooked up with him for a couple of months until he finally up and left? I'd be... crushed. I've got to move on. I've *got* to." She swallowed hard, knowing as she said the words that they were absolutely true. "He doesn't want what I want. He's not for me."

"He's an idiot," Chloe muttered. "He might seem like a smart guy, but he's an idiot."

Jill couldn't help but chuckle, feeling better despite herself. "He's not really. There's no rule that says all guys have to want committed relationships. Or all women for that matter. He's always been honest about it. He's never tried to manipulate me or use me. At all. He just... won't budge."

"So what we need to do is help you move on," Michelle said. "You need to focus on someone other than Lucas."

Chloe nodded. "Is there anyone at all you've had your eye on?"

Jill gave a twisted little smile.

"There is!" Chloe gasped. "Who is it?"

"I've been talking to Hal again. I know we kind of drifted apart, but he's a really nice guy. I've been wondering if I should maybe try it again."

"Are you interested in him?" Michelle asked.

"Eh," Jill admitted. Before her friends could reply, she added, "But that's the problem. I'm not interested in anyone but Lucas. And I have to be. I *have* to be. I can't just sit around and... hope he'll change."

"No," Chloe agreed. "You should at least try to move on. If you like Hal well enough, it would be worth another try with him. At least he'd be a start."

141

"And you never know. Maybe Hal's been the one for you all this time, and you just got tangled up with Lucas on your way to someone else." That was Michelle, sounding as encouraging as Jill had been with her earlier.

Jill hoped it was true, but at the moment she couldn't believe it.

Getting tangled up with Lucas had been one of the best things in her whole life.

She wanted to stay tangled up with him—forever if he'd let her.

But she wasn't going to pour herself out for a man who would only give her pieces of himself.

She'd done that once.

And she already knew that Lucas had the power to crush her far more completely than Ted ever had.

He wouldn't mean to. He would never intend to hurt her.

But he'd end up doing it anyway.

~

The following Saturday, Jill had a date.

With Hal—whom Lucas had thought was out of her life for good.

But somehow the guy had weaseled his way back in, and Jill was letting him do it.

Jill mentioned the date as she ate her cereal on Saturday morning. She mentioned it as if it were no big deal.

Lucas hadn't been expecting it, and he'd asked a bunch of questions about how and why this date had developed. He'd kept asking until Steve had finally told him to get a grip and leave Jill alone. It was just a fucking date.

Steve was right. Jill had every right to go out with anyone she wanted.

But Lucas hated the idea.

He hated the idea so much he brooded about it all day.

He'd been hoping she might decide to have sex with him again soon, but clearly her thoughts were drifting in another direction.

Hal's direction—with his too-long hair and his hipster glasses and his obvious adoration of Jill.

If she dated him this time, it was going to take. Lucas knew it as surely as he knew the moment his life had changed two years ago. She would end up marrying him. She'd kick the rest of them out of this apartment and share it with Hal instead. They'd end up having a couple of kids to fill the other bedrooms.

She'd have what she wanted. A forever home. A forever man. A forever family.

And Lucas would never be part of it.

He stayed at the gym for almost three hours that day, trying to work off his angst and get his head on straight again.

He should care about what was best for Jill, and Hal was obviously it.

Lucas couldn't give her what she needed.

Lucas would never deserve her.

It was better this way. He knew it was.

Lucas was going to be leaving town in a couple of months, and he would never look back.

But he still hated it.

He hated every part of it.

He hated the picture of Jill with Hal, the image he couldn't get out of his mind.

So he was dead on his feet from working himself to exhaustion in the gym and still stewing about Jill's upcoming date at almost seven that evening when she was getting ready.

Michelle was taking a bath, and Steve was sitting on a couch with his laptop.

Lucas had been sitting too, staring blindly at the television, while Jill puttered about getting ready.

She was dressed up for Hal. She was wearing a sexy little dress and her high socks with the pink bows on them.

Lucas bristled at the sight.

She'd worn those socks the first night they'd had sex.

It felt like they should be only for him.

He was giving himself a mental lecture to be good, to not say a word, to not get in her way. But when she came into the kitchen, searching the countertop for something, Lucas got to his feet.

His muscles ached from too much exercise, but he ignored them. He walked into the kitchen. "What are you looking for?"

"My earrings with the pink and silver beads on them. Have you seen them?"

"No."

"I thought I might have taken them off the other day when I was sitting here, but I can't find them anywhere." She gave the counter one last scan with her eyes but then evidently gave up. She looked back up at Lucas and was evidently surprised that he was standing so close to her.

Very close.

Almost trapping her against the counter.

"Oh no," she said, her voice very low. "Don't you dare."

"Don't I dare what?" His voice was more guttural than it should have been but just as soft as hers.

"Don't you dare do this again. Get all bristly and possessive. I'm going out with Hal, Lucas. I'm doing it."

"I know you are." He told himself to back up, but he couldn't seem to follow through. She smelled so good, so much like Jill, and every part of her was deliciously touchable.

But he wasn't allowed to touch.

"It's going to happen this time," she said, her eyes almost fierce as she met his gaze.

"Maybe," he said. "Or maybe you'll decide he's boring and you'll come back and fall in bed with me."

Her cheeks flushed, but her eyes narrowed. "I'm not doing that anymore," she murmured, so softly there was no way Steve could hear across the room. "Sex with you was good, but it wasn't enough for me. I told you that from the beginning. You can't be surprised or offended that I'm moving on at last."

Lucas was all wound up again. His heart was hammering, and adrenaline was coursing through his veins. It was taking all the control he possessed not to grab her and kiss her and fuck her right there against the counter. He wanted to so much. "I'm not surprised. Or offended."

"Then why are you standing there bristling about it?"

"Am I supposed to be happy? We had an arrangement."

"What arrangement?" she snapped, so angry now she spoke a little too loud. Evidently realizing it, she continued more softly, "You think that was a good arrangement for me? Here I am in all my manly glory. You get to fuck occasionally if you feel like it, but you don't get anything else

145

from me. Was I supposed to swoon that you offered me even that little bit?"

"No, you weren't supposed to swoon," Lucas growled. "What kind of asshole do you think I am?"

"I think you're the kind of asshole who's looming over me right now, all bristly that I'm going out with another man, when he's never offered me anything he knows I want. That's the kind of asshole I think you are."

Lucas blinked, the truth of what she was saying hitting him unexpectedly. He would have taken a step back so he wasn't cornering her this way, but he was momentarily frozen.

Jill was on a roll. "Do you want to be my boyfriend, Lucas?"

He stared at her, paralyzed by the question, paralyzed by the answer—the true answer—that had sprung immediately into his mind.

Yes. That was what he wanted.

"That's what I thought," she hissed, before he could get anything said. "You don't want to be my boyfriend. You don't want anything from me but sex. And it's not enough for me. You know it. You've always known it. And I'm not going to change my mind and suddenly decide that sex without any feelings is going to make me happy. It's not going to make me happy, and it never will. So I'm going out with Hal tonight. And I'm going to move on from this thing with you. I'm going to have sex with Hal. I'm going to *do* it, Lucas. Tonight. So you better rein in your horses and figure out how to accept it. Act like a decent human being, and let me try to find something and someone who is able to make me happy. Because it's never going to be you. It's *never* going to be you!" She sucked in a ragged breath before she added, "Please."

He was still frozen, still staring at her blindly. Her pretty face and angry eyes blurred slightly and never grew clear again.

He did manage to take a step back eventually, and Jill ducked her head and hurried out of the kitchen.

She'd never found her earrings.

Lucas stood there in front of the counter for minute after minute. He was still standing there when Jill came through again, calling out a general goodbye and that they shouldn't be worried if she wasn't back until morning.

She didn't really look at Lucas again.

She was going to have sex with Hal.

She'd meant what she said.

Lucas had really lost her—even the small pieces of her he'd had up until this point.

She was just... gone.

Taken from his life the way anything good could be taken, at any moment, without any warning.

"Hey," a voice came from behind him. "Hey, are you all right?"

Steve. He'd come into the kitchen at some point. Lucas had no idea when. He looked at Steve blankly.

"Shit," Steve muttered. "I know it sucks, but it's your own fault. What do you expect her to do?"

This.

Lucas expected her to do exactly this.

Steve made a face. "Okay. Well, let's not just sit around here all night. Let's go out, and I'll buy you a drink." He clapped Lucas on the shoulder. "Or maybe three."

Three sounded better than one.

However many drinks it would take to dull the endless ache he was feeling, to fill this emptiness that was tearing him apart.

That was how many drinks he needed.

~

Despite what she'd told Lucas, Jill didn't end up having sex with Hal that night.

She wanted to. She really wanted to want Hal that way, want any man other than Lucas.

But she didn't.

It wouldn't have been fair to Hal for her to use him that way, and it wouldn't have been good to herself to do something she didn't want just to prove that she could.

So she had dinner with Hal and said good night at the restaurant, walking the half block back by herself a little after eleven that evening.

She wondered what Lucas was doing.

She hoped he was okay.

He'd looked really hurt—dazed—by what she'd said to him earlier. Even if it had been true and necessary, she wished she'd been nicer about it.

She hadn't wanted to hurt him.

He'd been hurt enough in the past. He'd been hurt so badly.

She was confused by what she saw when she approached the apartment.

Steve's car was right out front in the loading zone, and he and Michelle were both standing on the sidewalk, staring in at the open door to the back seat.

"What's the matter?" Jill asked, speeding up as she grew closer. "What's going on?"

"Oh. Jill." Michelle gave her a flustered smile as she approached but then turned back to stare into the back seat of the car.

Jill was close enough now to see.

"Oh God!" she gasped. "Is he okay?"

Lucas was stretched out on the back seat of the car, face down and half hanging off the edge of the seat.

"He's drunk off his ass," Michelle whispered. "He can't even walk."

"I... can... too... walk," Lucas announced from the car. "I'm getting... up. Now." He didn't move.

"What happened?" Jill asked, hugging her arms to her chest and looking from Steve to Michelle. "How did he get this way?"

"We went to a bar," Steve explained. "He was... upset... about things. So I took him out. He kept drinking. I guess I should have stopped him, but he's always been able to handle his liquor. I don't know what happened. Damn, what a mess."

Jill's mind and heart were whirling. She'd never seen Lucas look so helpless, so completely out of it. She was terrified that she had somehow done it to him. "Do you think he's okay? I mean, we don't need to take him to the emergency room or someth—"

"I think he just needs to sleep it off," Steve said. "I need to get him upstairs." He reached into the back seat and tugged on Lucas's shirt. "Make an effort here, man. You're embarrassing yourself, and you're going to hate it tomorrow morning."

It was a bit of a process, but Lucas finally managed to stumble out of the car. He couldn't stand up straight, so Steve supported him on one side.

Then suddenly it seemed to register with Lucas that Jill was standing on the sidewalk next to Michelle.

He made a hissing sound. "Why aren't you out there..." He flailed one arm wildly. "Why aren't you out there fucking your... forever man?"

Jill's face contorted briefly with emotion.

This was about her after all.

"Shut the hell up and start walking," Steve told him. "We've got to get up the stairs."

Lucas was so out of it that Steve could barely keep him up, and Jill couldn't stand to see him looking so pitiful. So she hurried over and supported Lucas from the other side, and that made it easier for him to move forward.

Lucas leaned on her heavily, smelling strongly of whiskey. "What about your... forever man?" he kept asking as they slowly made their way up the stairs.

At one point, they had to stop because Lucas started to gag. He didn't throw up anything. Just made the choking sounds. It was awful. He was never like this.

Never so helpless, so out of control.

Eventually he was able to start moving again, and they finally reached the landing to their apartment.

Michelle opened the door, and they got Lucas inside, through the living room, and into his room where they could finally let him drop onto the small bed.

Lucas lay where he landed, breathing harshly with his eyes open.

He looked so uncomfortable that Jill reached down to try to reposition him, lifting the arm that was hanging over the side up onto the mattress.

Lucas grabbed her forearm. "Jill. Jill."

"What?" she asked.

"Where is... where is..."

He was still trying to ask about Hal.

There was no other explanation than that he'd fallen into this drunken mess because she'd gone out with Hal, because she'd told him she was going to sleep with him, because she'd told him she was moving on from him for good.

She couldn't believe he had reacted this way, that he'd gone to these lengths in response.

Steve had said he'd been upset.

He must have been *really* upset.

He hadn't even wanted her. Not in any real way. He'd just wanted to have sex with her.

Why would he have done this?

Practically in tears now, Jill tried to pull her arm away, but Lucas wouldn't give it up. He was holding on to it with a surprising amount of strength. He wasn't squeezing it. Just holding it.

She tried again. "Lucas, honey, let go." She tried prying off his fingers, but they wouldn't budge.

"Don't leave," Lucas mumbled. "Don't leave me."

Steve had gone to get a bottle of water and set it next to the bed, but now he saw what Jill was doing.

"Hey," he said sharply, leaning down to give Lucas a punch on the shoulder. "Let go of her. Let go."

Lucas grunted at the punch but didn't let go.

Steve reached for his hand, clearly intending to pry off his grip the way Jill had been trying to earlier but much less gentle than she'd been.

"Don't hurt him," Jill said, worried and bewildered and protective. Tears were streaming freely down her cheeks now.

"But he's hurting you."

"He's not hurting me. He's just holding on. It's not tight. He doesn't know what he's doing. He's just holding on." She adjusted so she was lying on the bed with him, turned on her side so Lucas could keep his grip on her forearm. He wasn't squeezing. She wasn't going to be bruised. He couldn't seem to relax his fingers. "It's fine. I'll just wait until he lets go."

"Are you sure?" Michelle asked. "Are you all right?"

"I'm all right. I want to... I want to stay here. He'll let go soon." Lucas had pulled her forearm toward him now, almost hugging it to his chest.

"Okay," Steven said, sounding a little dubious. "If he pukes all over you, don't blame me."

"He's not going to puke. He's not just drunk. He's... sad."

She knew as she said the final word that it was the true one.

Lucas wasn't just bristling and jealous. He wasn't just being a childish jackass.

He was sad.

He was broken.

And she didn't want him to be alone.

"Just call out if you need anything or if you need him to let go," Steve said, giving her a careful look as if to verify that she was really all right.

"I will," she told him. "I'm fine. I want to stay here with him."

"Okay. We'll be right across the hall," Michelle said as she and Steve started to leave.

Jill kicked off her shoes and adjusted to get a little more comfortable. The only way she could lie was on her side, facing Lucas, who was still clinging to her forearm like it was the only thing keeping him from drowning.

"Jill," he mumbled after another minute.

"I'm here."

"What about... your forever man?"

She let out a long sigh. "I found him. But he didn't want me forever."

Lucas didn't reply. She was pretty sure he hadn't followed what she'd said, and it was just as well.

She'd really expected him to release her arm after a few minutes. But he didn't.

Even after he appeared to fall asleep, he was still holding on to her.

Nine

Sometime during the night, Lucas had a brief flicker of consciousness. He knew that his head hurt and his mouth tasted like garbage and that every muscle in his body ached.

He also knew something else.

He knew Jill was in bed with him.

He couldn't see her, but he could feel her, smell her. He reached out and pulled her closer to him, wrapping both his arms around her little body.

He heard her give a soft, pretty moan as she snuggled against his chest. She was sleeping and clinging to him at the same time.

Letting out a slow breath, he relaxed again, holding her against him tightly.

It didn't matter that he felt terrible in almost every way.

Because Jill was here. He could touch her, hold her.

She hadn't slipped away yet.

When Lucas woke up for real, it was with the certain knowledge that he'd been a fool.

More than a fool. An embarrassing, immature, vulnerable fool.

A fool in front of his friends.

A fool in front of Jill.

He didn't even remember every detail, but he knew for sure that he'd blown it. Big time.

He didn't even want to open his eyes.

If he did, the sun would be up. The morning would have come. And he'd have to face up to what had happened last night.

He didn't want to do it.

Jill was still with him in bed. They'd moved during the night, and he wasn't on his side anymore, holding her against his front. She'd rolled over, and he'd rolled with her, so now he was half spooning her from behind and half lying on top of her.

He was still wearing the jeans and T-shirt he'd had on last night, and he was uncomfortably hard in his pants, his erection pressed up against the zipper. His brain pounded against his skull, and he needed to pee so badly he was in serious danger of losing it.

That was the thought that prompted him to finally open his eyes, roll away from Jill's small, sleeping body, and heave himself painfully out of bed.

The apartment was quiet as he walked across the hall to the bathroom.

After he'd gone, he splashed water on his face and returned the bedroom, where he shucked his jeans and T-shirt and dropped them onto the floor. In just his underwear, he returned to the bed and found the bottle of water on the box he was using as a nightstand.

He sat on the edge of the bed and drank down most of the bottle in several large gulps.

Jill was still sleeping, curled up on her side. Her hair was loose and falling into her face. She wore the sexy little dress she'd worn for her date with Hal the night before. She still had on her high socks.

His heart lurched, like it was literally reaching toward her, trying to get to her, trying to take hold of her.

He sat like a statue on the side of the small bed, making himself breathe slowly. He finished the last swallow of water.

Then he got up, went back to the bathroom to pee yet again, and then went to the refrigerator to grab another bottle of water.

When he returned to the room this time, Jill had turned over onto her back.

As he approached the bed, her eyes opened just a slit.

He sat down, looking at her quietly.

"You okay?" she asked hoarsely.

He opened his mouth to tell her he was fine.

Instead, he heard himself saying, "I don't know."

She lifted one hand, extending it toward him. He took it instinctively, automatically, letting her pull him back down onto the bed. He adjusted their bodies so she was pressed into his side, one of his arms holding her close.

"What happened last night," Jill asked after a few minutes. He'd thought maybe she'd gone back to sleep, but she hadn't.

"I... don't even know."

"Do you remember anything?"

"Yeah. Enough. Too much." He swallowed hard. "God, what a fool I am."

She didn't object to that sentiment. She must have known it was true as much as he did.

He couldn't help but stroke her hair with his free hand. It was soft and messy and draping over her face and shoulder. She sighed against him, as if she liked how it felt.

"I thought..." she began after another minute or two. "I thought you didn't want... you didn't want anything from me. But sex." Her words were stilted, and he could tell she was uncomfortable saying them.

She'd always been honest. Far more honest than he'd ever been.

"That's all I was supposed to want," he managed to say.

She lifted her head slightly so she could meet his eyes. "So you want... more?"

He heard the slight note of hope in her voice, and it wounded him.

It wounded him.

She wanted him still—no matter how much of a fool he'd always been.

There was no way in the world he deserved her.

"Yes," he admitted since she was waiting for his answer. "Of course I do. But I don't know..."

He didn't finish because there was too much lurking in the remainder of that sentence.

He didn't know if he could offer her more.

He didn't know if he was capable of more.

He didn't know if his scars had healed enough.

He didn't know if he would ever be able to follow through on what he wanted again.

"Tell me what you don't know, Lucas," Jill said, her voice so incredibly gentle.

He took a shaky breath. "I don't know if I'm... me anymore."

He hadn't meant to say that. He didn't even know what it meant. He'd broken out in a cold sweat, and he was staring up at the ceiling blindly.

Jill pulled out of his arm, turning over as she sat up so she was leaning over him. Her blond hair slid forward over her shoulders, and the neckline of her dress drooped, exposing a pretty pink lace bra and her lovely rounded breasts.

Lucas's body sprang to attention, but his mind and heart were too full to pay much attention to it at the moment. He was waiting to hear what she would say.

"Of course you're you," she murmured thickly, stroking his chest with one hand. "Lucas, why wouldn't you be you?"

He couldn't look away from her eyes. "Because I've spent all this time trying to be someone different, someone... stronger, safer. I've spent so much time trying to leave the man I was behind."

"Why, Lucas? What was so wrong with the man you used to be."

"He... got hurt." The words were forced out of his throat in a harsh rasp.

"Everyone gets hurt. It doesn't mean you can't still be you. Can't you... can't you show me the man you were before? I want to know him too. I want to be with him too."

His breath was coming out in ragged pants now, and he was sweating even more than he'd been before. There was a throbbing in his head that completely overwhelmed his headache. It was a throbbing he could feel against his skull and in his groin, but it was centered somewhere else.

It was centered in his heart.

He reached out for her. There was no way he could stop himself.

He pulled her over on top of him, and she came willingly.

Then he was kissing her, and her mouth was opening to his tongue, and every molecule in his body was screaming that this was right, she was his.

He was hers.

He wasn't in fit shape to think clearly or work through the best way to please her the way he normally did. He couldn't do anything but grope for her, hold on to her, desperately cling to her. His tongue was sliding against hers but not with any strategy or skill. His hands were moving all over her, feeling her soft flesh, lush curves, dips and edges and textures. And his erection was so hard now it was causing his whole body to pulse. He kept groaning into her mouth. Loudly. Uninhibited.

She seemed just as uncontrolled as he was. She was straddling his hips and rubbing herself against him eagerly—with her whole body. Her fingernails were gouging holes into one of his shoulders and the back of his neck from how tightly she was clutching at him. And she was making little whimpers and grunts that were driving him absolutely wild.

Before he knew what was happening, he'd dragged the dress off over her head, and she'd pulled off his underwear. One or both of them had managed to remember the condom, and she was rolling it on for him. Then he was guiding her hips over him, and she was sheathing him in the warm, wet clasp of her body.

He groaned loud and long at the sheer pleasure of it. Like a boy, like a horny teenager. She was already trying to ride him, so far gone that she was flushed red and panting out a building rhythm.

He took her hips in a firm grip and started to buck up into her.

They had no steady rhythm between them. No unified motion. Both of them were out of control, frantically clinging to the other as the sensations overwhelmed them.

"Lucas," she was crying out. "Oh, Lucas, please. Please, please, please, please. I need... I need... you." She kept babbling out the words as she rode him with shameless abandon.

He'd never seen anything more beautiful. More pure.

Just the sight of her, the sound of her, was enough to snap any remaining threads of his control. He moaned again—over and over again—as his hips bucked up into her helplessly. He couldn't have held them still even if he'd wanted to.

And he didn't want to.

He wanted to let loose completely. Just like this. He wanted to give her everything. He didn't want to hold anything back.

She was sobbing as she came, her body clenching and shuddering as her head fell back in pleasure. Her internal muscles squeezed around him so hard that he roared with it, his climax hitting him fast and hard.

He rocked beneath her, wild and unrestrained, shaking the bed, shaking his whole world.

She collapsed down on top of him when the spasms were finally spent, and he held her close.

Just as close as he'd been holding her before.

He needed her now just as much.

She squirmed a few times on top of him, as if her body were still reveling in her orgasm. Then she lifted up her head and smiled down at him.

He knew he was smiling too.

Like a fool.

"I knew I would like him," she whispered, pressing a little kiss against his lips.

"Who?" He really had no idea what she was talking about.

"The old you. The man you used to be. I knew I would like him too."

The words saturated him with pleasure. Warm, bone-deep pleasure. But they also made an ache in his chest tighten until he could hardly breathe around it. He gently pried her loose from his body and rolled her over onto her side. He made a bit of a mess with the condom, but he managed to tie it off.

Then he stood up.

He knew Jill was watching him. He knew that what he did right now mattered.

He knew it mattered more than anything.

He couldn't look at her. He grabbed his underwear and walked across the hall to the bathroom.

It was still early on a Sunday morning. Michelle and Steve weren't up yet.

Jill was waiting in his bedroom, in his bed.

And what happened next would change everything.

He was terrified.

He was so terrified he was breathing in loud, uneven gasps.

He threw away the condom. Cleaned himself up. Splashed water on his face. Stared at himself in the mirror.

He looked the way he always did. He needed to shave. He needed a haircut. He needed to put a shirt on.

He had a long, ugly scar down his back.

He wasn't the man he used to think he was.

161

He wasn't a man who had it all together.

He was going to make a mess of this and hurt Jill unforgivably in the process.

The man she wanted was a man who had never really existed.

He had no idea how long he stood there, staring into the mirror, but eventually he heard a light tap on the bathroom door.

Making himself turn away from the mirror, he reached to open the door.

It was Jill, wearing nothing but one of his T-shirts. She gazed up at him with huge blue eyes. Wary eyes. Like she knew something bad was coming.

It was coming.

It would slam into them without warning. The way it had slammed into Lucas two years ago.

Knocking him off his feet.

Ripping his body apart.

Proving he had no power over anything that mattered.

It was going to slam into him again. In exactly the same way.

Jill didn't say anything. She just took his arm and pulled him back into the bedroom. She closed the door behind them and led Lucas back to the bed.

He sat down when his legs buckled.

She sat down next to him.

He stared at the old hardwood floors, worn into warm, rich color from age and use and craftsmanship. From years of supporting the weight of human lives.

Some things were like that.

Some things could stand the test of time and grow stronger and more beautiful because of it.

Some things didn't break.

"Lucas," Jill said, folding her legs up underneath her and leaning against him. "You need to talk to me."

He took a hoarse breath, and to his dismay, it sounded almost like a sob.

Jill made a soft, little whimper. She reached an arm around his back and let her fingers trace along the line of his scar.

It was like she was trying to make it better.

But it couldn't be made better.

It would never go away. Not even when he took his final breath.

"Lucas," she whispered. "Please, honey. Tell me."

He knew he needed to do it.

He'd spent so long telling himself that no one would really understand, but he somehow knew she would.

She would understand.

The truth wouldn't change what she felt for him.

But he didn't know why she felt that way in the first place.

He made another choked sound in his throat with the effort to get something—anything—said.

After a minute, Jill drooped beside him. She was still leaning against him, still had her arm around him. But she seemed to have accepted the inevitable.

She was crying, he realized with another slash of pain through his heart.

"Lucas," she said at last, wiping some of the tears away. "I know you're going through a lot of really hard stuff. I don't know what it is, but I think I can understand. You don't have to tell me everything right now. You really don't."

The words should have relieved the crippling burden he was carrying, but they didn't.

They made him feel worse, more guilty, more completely helpless.

He reached behind him to take the arm she'd been stroking him with, pulling it back around to the front of his body so she was no longer touching his scar.

"But..." Jill cleared her throat. "I do need to know... I need to know if there's any hope for us. If you could ever... ever want to be in a real relationship with me. I don't mean to give you an ultimatum or anything like that. I promise I don't. But it feels like I'm pouring myself out here. I keep pouring myself out. And I still don't know... I still don't know if it's even something you... you want."

He did want it.

Desperately.

Never in his life had he ever wanted something so much.

But that didn't mean it would be right to take it.

He was still holding on to her forearm, his fingers wrapped around her delicate bones. She seemed so small. He could hurt her.

Maybe he already had.

He couldn't loosen his grip.

"Lucas," Jill prompted when he still didn't answer. "You can't do this to me. It's not... it's not right. You don't have to tell me everything right now. We don't have to work everything out right away. But you need to tell me this at least. Is there even a chance?"

He managed to turn his head and look at her instead of at the floor. She was still crying. And he was still holding her forearm in an inexorable grip.

They stared at each other for a long time, and then he saw something change on her face.

Resignation.

An aching kind of acceptance.

"Okay," she whispered at last. "Okay. If there's no chance, then you need to... you need to let me go. We can't do this anymore. Not any of it. Because it's... it's breaking me."

Of course it was breaking her. It had already broken him.

"It's breaking my heart," she said. "And I can't just let it keep happening. You've always been a decent guy with me. You really have. You've treated me like a human being. You've respected my choices. You've cared about how I was feeling. You've been decent, Lucas. So you need to be decent one more time. You need to let me go now." She gave a brief, helpless sob before she added, "Everything is what I want. I want a... a real home, a man who will love me forever. So if you know you'll never be able to give me everything, then you need to let me go."

An aching, needy voice deep inside Lucas was screaming, howling, begging for this not to happen. But Jill was weeping now—small and hurt and so incredibly sad—and it was all because of Lucas.

So he used every last thread of strength he possessed, and he managed to loosen his fingers, break the grip he had on her forearm.

He strangled on a wordless sound as his hand finally let her go.

Jill sobbed as she pulled her arm toward her chest. She sat for a minute, gazing at Lucas with tear-filled eyes. Then she jumped up and ran out of the room.

Lucas let her.

That little voice inside him was still wailing its outrage to the heavens, but his body didn't move.

Jill was right.

He couldn't be the man she needed him to be.

So he couldn't be her man at all.

~

Jill cried in her bedroom for more than an hour, and then she finally fell asleep in an exhausted heap. The night had been too long, and the emotional toll had been too heavy.

This was really the end, and she knew it.

It was almost ten in the morning when she woke up again. Her eyes ached, and she was sick to her stomach. She got up, used the bathroom, washed her face, and put a sweatshirt on over Lucas's T-shirt, which she was still wearing.

Then she steeled her nerve and walked out into the common room of the apartment.

She had no idea what she would say when she saw Lucas again.

She had no idea about anything.

She went first for the coffee, but she recognized that the vibes in the apartment were strange, different. Michelle was working on her laptop at the counter, and Steve was lounging on the couch with a newspaper. But something was different.

Really different.

Really wrong.

She met Michelle's eyes over her coffee cup.

Michelle's face twisted strangely. "Are you all right?"

Jill tried to answer, but couldn't.

Steve had sat up now. Both he and Michelle were watching her with heavy, anxious expressions.

Finally Jill shrugged, trying to clear her throat so she could answer for real.

Then something suddenly occurred to her.

It hit her with a flash of painful insight.

She put her coffee cup down on the counter and walked out of the kitchen. Through the main room to the hallway. Then down two doors to Lucas's room.

His door was open.

She stood in the doorway.

She saw what was inside.

Nothing.

The bedroom was empty—nothing but a bare mattress on a cheap twin frame. All of Lucas's possessions were gone.

Lucas was gone.

She stared blindly at the empty room, and it somehow embodied exactly how her heart felt right now.

Just... empty.

"I'm so sorry, Jill," Michelle said softly from behind her. "He was almost entirely packed when we woke up this morning. Then he just... he just left."

Jill managed to give her head a stiff nod.

Of course he had.

He was trying to be decent.

He was trying to do as she'd asked.

He was trying to let her go.

Ten

Lucas had packed up his room and left that morning, convinced he was never coming back.

That was how it worked with him now.

He stayed until things happened to him, and then he took off.

Things had happened here in Blacksburg, and now it was time to leave. He'd packed his car. He'd left a check to cover more than his share of the last two months of utilities. He'd walked out the front door, gotten into the driver's seat, and pulled out onto the road.

He drove out of town, taking 460 to Christiansburg. Then he took the ramp to I-81 toward Roanoke. He didn't know where he was going. He was just getting away.

He'd made Jill cry earlier like her heart was breaking.

He wasn't going to do it again.

There wasn't much traffic this early on a Sunday morning, just a lot of tractor trailers going way too fast down the mountain. He maneuvered around most of them. He was driving fast too.

When he got to the next exit, he pulled off the interstate without putting on his turn signal.

He didn't even know why.

Responding to an unstoppable force that was controlling his actions, he turned around and drove back to Blacksburg.

He ended up downtown, and he circled until he found a parking spot on the street from which he could see the apartment building.

He didn't get out.

He didn't go up.

He just sat in his car and waited.

He had no idea what he was doing, but he couldn't seem to drive away again.

He sat there for more than two hours, watching people stroll by, enjoying their Sundays, stopping in shops, grabbing a bite to eat, smiling and laughing and living their lives as if they couldn't be torn away from them at any moment.

He saw Jill's boss and his sister walk across the street and go into Tea for Two. Jill worked with both of them. She liked both of them. She said they had really good hearts.

That mattered to Jill—more than anything else.

She'd thought he had a good heart too.

He'd thought he had one too... a long time ago.

He kept sitting, waiting, watching. Eventually he saw Chloe striding down the sidewalk like she was on a mission. She was wearing a pair of loud red leggings and a long, off-the-shoulder top. She wasn't smiling.

She pressed the buzzer next to the exterior door, and after a minute she walked into the apartment building.

She was going to visit Jill.

Jill was upstairs.

Lucas could reach her in less than three minutes, if he just got out of his car.

He didn't move.

After a while, the door to the apartment building opened again. Chloe came out first. She was obviously talking because her lips were moving and her expression was animated.

Jill followed her, dressed in jeans and a white top. Her hair was pulled back in a low ponytail.

It was the simplest outfit he'd ever seen her wear. It didn't look like her at all.

Her head was turned behind her, and she held the door for Michelle and then Steve.

They all stood on the sidewalk for a minute, talking about something. Then Chloe went into Tea for Two, followed by Jill. After a moment, Michelle dragged Steve inside too.

He didn't object, although he was clearly putting up an exaggerated fuss about going into the girly little shop.

He went in though.

He was doing it for Jill. Lucas knew it instinctively.

All of them were there for Jill—because they thought she was sad, because they wanted to cheer her up.

Jill thought of them like family.

They were home to her.

For a while Lucas had felt part of it too.

He wanted it.

All of it.

All of them.

He wanted Jill so much it was strangling him.

Instead, he had... nothing.

It felt like he was drowning, like he literally couldn't breathe.

He fumbled in the passenger seat until he got his hand on his phone. Without thinking, he dialed the only number he could think of to dial.

He waited as it rang.

"Hello? Lucas? Is that you?" The familiar voice was surprised, hopeful.

"Yeah, Mom," he said, trying to make his voice sound natural. "It's me."

"What's wrong?"

"Nothing is wrong. I just called to say hi."

"Why are you lying to me?"

Lucas sat behind the steering wheel, staring blindly at a group of college kids crossing the road in front of him. His hand was shaking, and he didn't know why.

"Lucas, did something happen?" his mother asked, sounding strangely gentle.

"N-no."

She paused for a moment. "You can tell me about it."

He didn't answer. He couldn't.

"I know you think we've never understood, but we do. We really do. You almost died. You came so close. We know things would feel different after that. We don't think you're overreacting. You don't have to hide from us."

He had been. Hiding from everything, everyone, anyone who might make him feel too much, might threaten the artificial peace he'd created in his heart.

He didn't want to hide anymore. Not from his family.

Not from Jill.

When he didn't respond, his mother went on, "You know you can come home any time you want. To stay or just to visit or whatever you want. Do you want to come home?"

His throat had constricted so much his breathing was loud and hoarse. "Yes," he managed to say in an embarrassing rasp. "I want to come home."

"Then come. Come right now. We miss you so much."

He was shaking so much now he could barely hold the phone steady. "I might..." When his voice cracked, he had to start again. "I might bring someone with me, if that's all right."

"Of course it is!" Her tone had changed. She was clearly both surprised and pleased by that piece of information. "We would love that. You know we would. You bring anyone you want, anyone who's special to you. It doesn't matter to us who they are."

"I don't know... I don't know if she'll come. I didn't treat her..." He took a ragged breath as the truth hit him hard. "I didn't treat her right."

His mom said, "Well, maybe she'll forgive you if you tell her the truth. Just make sure you treat her right from now on."

~

Jill had a very bad morning.

Despite her friends' attempts to comfort and encourage her, the morning dragged on and on. They went down to Tea for Two and bought almost every kind of goodie Carol had made that morning, splurging on the most expensive tea. Chloe, Michelle, and Steve were all trying to keep the mood light, to make her laugh.

And she appreciated it. A lot.

But she was exhausted when they went back up to the apartment, and Jill just didn't have the energy to keep trying to be all right. So she said she needed a nap.

She thought she would cry alone in her room, but she was too drained to even cry.

She got under the covers and actually went to sleep.

She couldn't remember the last time she'd gone sound asleep at one o'clock in the afternoon, but she was totally out of it.

So out of it that she was aware of nothing—nothing at all—until she felt someone's hand on her shoulder.

It jarred her awake.

Then she became aware of someone sitting on the edge of her bed, leaning over her, touching her.

She gasped and sat up straight so quickly she knocked her forehead against the other person's head.

She huffed at the impact, raising a hand to the bump on her temple.

"Ouch," Lucas said, raising one of his hands in exactly the same way she was.

Lucas.

It was Lucas.

In her bedroom.

Sitting on her bed.

Lucas.

"I'm sorry," he said. "I didn't know you were really asleep."

"What did you think I was doing in here?" She was dazed and not really following what was happening.

"I thought were... I didn't mean to wake you up."

"Well, you did."

Then the reality finally caught up to her.

Lucas was here when he shouldn't be.

He really shouldn't be.

"Oh no, no, no, no, no." She was still covering the painful spot on her head, but something much worse than that was hurting now too. "Lucas, you can't be here. You were going to let me go. You were going to be a decent man."

"I know," he said, the strangest expression on his face. It was twisted, like he was feeling too much to hold on to with his normal composure. "I know I was going to do that. But I don't want to be just a decent man. I want to be... better. I want to be... good."

She gasped, still holding her head. She stared at him, trying to understand, trying to contain a surge of hope that was suddenly flooding her heart, her chest, her whole body. "What... what do you mean?"

"I mean I want to be good." His green eyes were soft, almost tender, completely vulnerable. "I want to..." He cleared his throat. "I'm so sorry I hurt you."

"You... you are?"

"Yes. I'm so sorry. I was so..."

"So what?" she whispered, her head and heart and vision all spinning. These weren't just words he was saying to smooth over a conflict. She could see they were real. His face was twisting with emotion.

"So scared. Because what I have with you is so... real."

"I thought it was too," she admitted, wiping a stray tear from her cheek.

"I spent so long trying not to feel helpless, trying not to feel weak. But that's what I've been with you. I don't want to be that anymore." He paused. "I'm going to go home for a few days—back to Iowa. I want to see my folks. And I need to... I need to face up to a few things."

Her hand moved down to cover her heart. "I think that's a good idea," she said softly.

She still didn't know what was happening here, but she was sure it had to be good for Lucas.

He'd been riding the tide, letting things happen to him for too long.

He needed to face what had hurt him so he could finally heal.

"Will you..." Lucas's hoarse voice trailed off. He stared down at his hand on her covers and then slanted a look back up to her. "Would you like to go with me?"

Her breath hitched. She sat perfectly still.

"I understand if you don't want to," he said when she didn't answer. "I'm going to go regardless. But I thought... I want to tell you some stuff. I should have done it earlier. I shouldn't have kept holding back on you. I was wrong. I was scared. But I want to be... better. And I really want to be with you. For real this time."

A single tear slid out of her eye, down her cheek, and then plopped onto the sheet. "I would love to go with you, Lucas," she said. "I just need to ask my boss if I can take a couple of days off. Did you want to go right away?"

"I did," Lucas said. "But I'll wait for you if it needs to be later."

She reached for her phone. "Let me call him and see. He was down in Tea for Two earlier."

~

Patrick was fine with her taking a couple of days off since she was caught up on her work and didn't currently have any pressing deadlines, so she and Lucas drove to Roanoke and got on a plane. By the evening, they were in Des Moines.

The whole thing was happening so fast that Jill could barely keep up.

She knew Lucas was serious. She knew he'd turned some kind of corner. He hadn't promised her anything yet, but she knew it was coming.

He'd made mistakes, but he wasn't a bad man. He wasn't selfish. And he wouldn't be doing this with her now unless it meant something, unless he was ready to commit.

She trusted him. She didn't have to have all the compartments of her life perfectly tidy to know this was what she wanted. *Lucas* was who she wanted.

So she didn't push him. She was going to wait until he was ready.

Lucas rented a car at the airport, and she thought they would go straight to his parents'. But they were both hungry, so they stopped and got some sandwiches to eat. Then Lucas drove through downtown, stopping in front of an office building.

"What's this?" she asked since he was staring at the building like it was significant.

"This is where I used to work."

"Oh really?" She peered at the place, but it wasn't anything noteworthy. Just a generic office building, like thousands of other ones. "Did you really hate it?"

"Not the work. Not all of it. But I did hate going to sit in an office every day. I just can't do that again."

"Well, maybe you can find another way to work."

He nodded. "That's what I'm going to do. I've already taken a bunch of jobs from friends of Steve and Michelle."

"You have?" She knew he would hear the surprise in her voice, but there was no way to disguise it.

"Yeah. I didn't tell anyone, but I've been doing that. I've liked working that way—just going over to people's homes and helping them out. I can work on building up a business that way."

"I think that's a great idea." She gave a little chuckle. "So all this time, you haven't been the slacker you pretended to be."

"Well," he admitted, "at first I was. I thought it would be easier that way—so I didn't have to work hard building something that might be taken away in the blink of an eye. But I guess I'm not really a slacker at heart."

She smiled at him, and he smiled back. And then he pulled the car away from the curb. He drove out of the downtown area and through several residential areas until he'd gotten to an older neighborhood with small brick houses and big yards. He took several turns until he pulled in front of a brick ranch with several big trees in the side yard and a concrete patio.

"Where are we now?" she asked.

"This was my house."

"It was?" She leaned forward, peering at the house. It wasn't a new build, but it was in good shape. The yard was well kept, and the overall look was comfortable and attractive. "I like it." She turned back toward him. "It looks like a nice little house. Did you like it?"

He let out a little breath. "Yeah. I did."

"Why did you sell it?"

"I didn't want to be that man anymore. The man who owned this house. I wanted to be... unfettered. I didn't want to pour myself into anything—even a house—that could be... taken away."

The words reflected what he'd said about his job. Taken away. Something had been taken away from him in the past. She felt a familiar knot of worry in her gut. It felt like something was coming. Something big. Something hard.

Without another word, Lucas pulled back onto the street. She knew from what he'd told her in the past that his parents lived somewhere near here, but he didn't go to their house. He drove out of the neighborhood and through a commercial area until he reached what looked like a park and community center. There was a baseball field and tennis courts in view.

Lucas parked the car and got out, so Jill got out with him.

She took his arm as they walked, and she could feel that he was shaking just a little.

He hadn't said anything since he'd left his old house.

He led them to a corner where two sidewalks met—at the intersection of two roads. There was a traffic light, and several cars were waiting for it to turn green so they could go.

Jill looked up at Lucas and waited.

He was breathing unevenly now, and the color had left his face. Something haunted was evident in his eyes.

She reached out to hold on to both his hands. She was nervous, almost terrified, but she didn't prompt him to continue. She waited until he was ready to speak.

He inhaled hoarsely and began, "I was on a baseball team for a community league. We had practice on Thursday nights. I was leaving. I was standing here. I'd been arguing with Carly, my fiancée, and I was bored with work, and I..."

When he trailed off, Jill squeezed his hands.

He went on. "I remember standing right here, thinking how I didn't really want my life. Nothing was making me happy. And then... and then... exactly then... an SUV ran the light right there. She was texting while she was driving, and she just drove right through on the red. She hit another car and then got propelled this way. She went over the curb, and I was standing here and..."

"Bam," Jill said, very softly.

Lucas swallowed so hard she could see it in his throat. "Bam. The SUV hit me so hard I got thrown all the way over there. There was a concrete block with a plaque on it, and a corner of it tore open my back. I almost died. I had to be resuscitated. I was in the hospital for almost a month. They say I came within a breath of dying, but I feel like I actually did. And afterward... I was terrified."

"Of course you were. After that kind of trauma."

"I had months of therapy afterward, and I tried to do everything I was supposed to do. Like a good boy. But I was still terrified. About everything. It felt like I had no control over anything. Like anything and everything could be taken away by something so... random."

"I can understand that." Her voice shook just slightly.

"So nothing I did seemed to matter. I didn't want to be the man I'd been before, the one who worked hard and took life seriously. If life was so... fragile, so uncertain, if it could be taken away so quickly, then what was the point of... of anything I'd been doing. It just made me weak and vulnerable. It just made it hard when life got ripped away."

Lucas was still white, still shaking slightly, and she knew just coming back here, just standing on this corner again, had been incredibly hard.

Harder than anything she could imagine.

She made a little wordless sound and pulled him into a hug.

He wrapped his arms around her tightly, holding on to her, not letting her go. She could feel emotion shuddering through him, and it was shuddering through her too.

He'd almost died.

He'd come so close.

Then she never would have met him at all.

She would have lived her entire life without touching him, seeing him, knowing him, loving him.

She'd almost lost him before he'd ever been hers.

When his arms finally loosened, he pulled back to meet her eyes. "Tell me the truth. Are you... disappointed?"

"*Disappointed?*" Her voice cracked on the one word.

"Because the bam wasn't as big as you thought it would be. Didn't you think it would be... horrific? Because I've spent so long making it so important."

"It *was* important! It was horrific. You almost died, Lucas. I can't even imagine what that felt like. I can understand why it changed you, even though I don't think it changed you as much as you believed."

He gave her a little smile, more color coming back to his face. "Maybe it didn't."

She went on. "I understand all of it. All of it. Except..."

"Except what?" He wiped away a stray tear from her face with his fingertips.

"Why couldn't you tell me what happened to you?"

He shook his head very slightly. "I don't know. It was all just... blocked. And I knew it was all irrational—how I was acting, what I'd taken from the accident. I knew it didn't make logical sense and that it would just prove I was weak and vulnerable and... foolish. I guess I was just... embarrassed, as stupid as that sounds."

She hugged him again. "Thank you for telling me."

"Thank you for waiting until I could."

~

When they finally got to Lucas's parents' house, Jill was exhausted and emotional. It felt like she'd lived several lifetimes since yesterday, and she met Lucas's parents and then the rest of his family, who all came over for dinner, in a daze.

A good daze, but definitely a daze.

His parents had a huge dining room table, and they added an extra leaf so everyone could squeeze around it as they ate barbecue pork, macaroni and cheese, cole slaw, and homemade rolls. The conversation was loud and excited, and there were too many people involved to have deep discussion.

Which was just as well.

If Jill had to have another deep discussion today, she would just burst into tears.

Lucas had been slightly awkward at first, slightly sheepish, as if he was embarrassed by how he'd been acting for the past two years.

She'd never seen him embarrassed about anything before, but she kind of liked that he was now.

It meant he loved his family.

It meant he cared about what they thought about him.

Everyone was obviously curious about her, but no one asked rude or intrusive questions, which she appreciated. They did act like she and Lucas were in a serious relationship, but she didn't actually mind that.

It made something inside her shudder in excitement.

When dinner was over, she helped with the dishes. She was standing at the sink, rinsing off plates before she loaded them into the dishwasher, when Lucas's sister came to stand beside her with several used glasses.

Jill smiled at the other woman, whose name was Laura. She was a few years older than Lucas, and she had his beautiful green eyes and was several months pregnant.

"You really don't have to help with all this," Laura said.

"I don't mind. I like to tidy things up."

Laura opened her mouth to reply, but something strange happened to her face. It contorted dramatically, and she closed her eyes and turned her head away from Jill.

"Are you all right?" Jill asked, immediately concerned.

"Yes, yes. I'm fine. Sorry. I'm just... just so happy." Laura's expression cleared, and she gave a wobbly smile. "My husband keeps telling me not to start bawling, but I'm just so happy. Lucas is back, and he seems... so much better."

Jill immediately understood how the other woman felt. "He's really great."

"I know he is. We all know he is. He's always been so... warm and generous and funny and... sweet. Everyone has always loved him. He always had so many friends, and he worked so hard at his job and on his house. I know he wanted to be a husband and father, and then..." Her voice broke, and she trailed off. She had to clear her throat before she continued, "He came so close to dying. I still have nightmares about it. And even then, he worked so hard at getting better. I thought he would be able to go back to... But as soon as he was better, he just left. I know he thought we were disappointed in him, that we didn't understand why he felt the need to be someone else. We wouldn't have cared if something else made him happy, except it seemed like he was just… running away."

Jill was listening intently, soaking in every word. "I don't think he is anymore."

"I know. That's why I'm so happy that my pregnant self can't stop blubbering about it. I haven't seen him like this—so genuine and so happy—in years." Then her tone changed, and she shot Jill a mischievous look. "And I've never seen him so in love. Not ever."

Jill sucked in a breath, although she couldn't help but like the sound of that. "I don't know—"

"I know. I've known Lucas for twenty-seven years. I've never seen him like this with any other woman. Ever."

Jill's cheeks were flushed, but there was no way she could help it. She felt ridiculously like giggling.

Before she could think of an appropriate response, a new voice came from the entrance to the kitchen. "You're not saying something embarrassing about me, are you?"

Both women turned to look at Lucas, who was half smiling but also arching his eyebrows questioningly.

"Well, I'm your big sister," Laura said. "I'm supposed to embarrass you."

Lucas came over, wrapping an arm around Jill and pulling her against him. The gesture felt natural, as did the way she put a hand on his shirt.

"What were you saying?" Lucas asked.

"I was about to tell her how you were that school play in seventh grade and fainted on stage." Laura's voice was light, and it was clear she wasn't going to admit what she'd really been talking about the moment before.

Jill said, "You really fainted?"

Lucas groaned, but he kept his arm around her.

~

Late that night, Lucas was so exhausted he could barely stay on his feet.

After dinner, his mom and dad insisted he and Jill stay in a guest room. Lucas wasn't sure whether Jill would be comfortable with that, but she hadn't seemed to mind.

It was almost eleven at night, and he was finally getting into bed. He'd taken a shower first, so Jill was already under the covers, waiting for him.

Lucas was so tired and emotionally drained he could barely speak.

But he wanted to make sure Jill was all right.

A lot had happened today.

And they still hadn't talked about some of the things they needed to say.

He rolled onto his side so he was facing her. He'd turned off the light as he came to bed, but there was light from the bedside clock and light from the crack under the door from the hallway, so he could just barely see Jill's face and the outline of her body.

"Are you okay?" Jill asked, reaching out to touch his chest.

"I was just about to ask you the same thing."

"I'm fine."

"I know my family is… a lot to take."

"I like them. And they seem so happy to see you. They must have missed you a lot."

"I missed them too," he admitted.

She didn't say anything else, but it seemed like she was staring at him in the dark.

He hoped things hadn't moved too fast for her. If she was scared away from a relationship with him, he wasn't sure what he'd do. He asked, "Are you sure you're all right, baby?"

"I'm..." She gave a little laugh. "I'm more than fine. I'm... happy."

He groaned in relief and pulled her against him, wrapping both arms around her. He buried his face in her hair.

"What about you?" she asked, her voice muffled by his bare chest.

"I'm tired," he told her. "And relieved. And embarrassingly emotional. And... kind of nervous. I don't have any idea what's going to happen now, but I care again. I care about it again. It's... an adjustment."

"Yeah. I guess it would be."

He nuzzled her neck. "But beneath all that, I'm happy too. Honestly, I didn't think I'd ever be this happy again."

Her arms tightened around him, and her hand moved along his back until it was tracing the line of his scar.

It felt so intimate it was almost uncomfortable. Lucas muttered softly, "You don't need to pet the thing."

She knew exactly what he was talking about. Exactly what he felt and why he felt it. "Yes, I do."

"I'm always going to hate the thing."

"I'm not."

That surprised him, so he pulled back enough to see her face. His vision had adjusted, so he could see her expression now. Her eyes were huge, and her mouth was trembling a little. "Why not?"

"Because you wouldn't be you without it."

For a moment his heart was so full he couldn't process it, couldn't contain it. When he was able speak, he said, "You know I love you, don't you?" he asked. "You know that's what all this means."

"I..." She giggled softly. "I'd hoped so."

A swell of joy was breaking now in his heart, overwhelming everything else. "Well, I do. I love you. I want to be your forever man, if you think... if you want me for that long."

She fell into half laughter, half sob as she grabbed for him and pulled him close again. "I do. Want you. Forever. You've always been my forever man. You're the only one I've ever wanted."

Lucas held her for a long time, clutching her in a hard grip that seemed to embody his deepest need. She was small and soft and warm and real, and she wasn't going to go away.

She made him vulnerable. She made him weak.

But she also made him strong.

And it was worth it. For however long he was allowed to have her, to love her, to hold her like this, it was worth it.

Maybe one day she'd get taken away from him, but it would never be by his choice. And he was going to hold on to her for as long as he could.

Eventually his body started to react to her closeness, and they made love in soft, urgent silence under the covers. He kissed her the whole time, and she wrapped her legs around him. He gave her everything he had, everything he had in him to give, and she took it, accepted it, wanted it, gave it back to him.

When he woke up the next morning, it felt like he'd been made new. He was excited about what the day would bring.

And maybe it wouldn't just be what happened to him. Maybe he could start making things happen again.

~

A couple of weeks later, Chloe came over on Friday evening, and they ate pizza and played Steve's silly party game again.

Jill couldn't remember ever having such a good time— her pleasure untainted by uncertainty or confusion.

She loved Lucas, and Lucas loved her, and they were starting to make a life together. Here in Blacksburg. In their loft apartment.

Maybe eventually they'd want to have a house of their own, but they weren't there yet. They both really liked it here, and they wanted to stay.

She and Lucas had been on a team together, against the other three. The score was neck and neck, and it was her and Lucas's turn to answer the final question.

She was standing on the couch for some reason—she had no idea why she'd gotten up—and she was leaning against Lucas's back, her arms wrapped around his neck.

She got the answer to the question right, and she was shouting in triumph as Lucas turned around, picked her up, and whirled her around. The others were moaning in exaggerated defeat, but eventually they all fell into laughter.

When the game was over, Jill got up to start picking up, and Lucas helped her by collecting bottles. He dumped them into recycling and then cornered her against the kitchen counter so he could kiss her for a few minutes.

She had no objections to that.

"Hey," Chloe called out from the living area. "I thought one of the rules of this apartment was that sex stayed in the bedroom."

"No one is having sex," Jill called back. Lucas's body was pressed up against hers, and he certainly had sex on his mind, if the bulge in the front of his pants was any indication.

"Are you sure? Because you know we can see you over here, right?"

Jill giggled and pushed Lucas away, murmuring to him, "We'll have to save that for later."

"Count on it," he said against her ear.

Chloe left a few minutes later, and Jill and Lucas finished cleaning up.

Michelle came back from the front door, where she'd been saying good night to Chloe, and she caught Jill near the refrigerator.

Michelle had appeared to have had a good time this evening, but there was something poignant in her eyes now. She whispered to Jill, "I've got to break up with him."

Jill froze, her heart dropping into her gut.

She was so happy, so settled, so at home. And she'd hoped it would last a little longer.

But change would always catch up with her, and no attempt to keep things safe and cozy would ever hold it back.

She reached out to squeeze Michelle's arm. "You're sure?"

Michelle nodded. "I have to."

Jill nodded, seeing the emotion her friend was trying to contain. Then she reached out to pull Michelle into a hug. "I'm here for you. No matter what."

Steve was on the couch, looking at his phone, looking like he had no idea what was about to happen to him. Jill could see him over Michelle's shoulder, and she ached for him.

Her eyes moved to Lucas. He was watching her, his expression sober, as if he realized that something was wrong.

He loved her, and he wasn't going anywhere.

Her world might change, but his place in it wouldn't.

He was hers now. For the long run.

The night she'd first met him, she'd thought he would be the perfect guy for a one-night stand.

But life never happened the way she thought it would, and it turned out he was the perfect guy for forever.

Epilogue

A month later, Jill came home to Michelle and Steve fighting. Again.

She'd hoped that their breaking up would bring an end to the fights, but it hadn't.

The problem was they were still living together.

It was early spring, a terrible time for apartment hunting in Blacksburg. So they'd agreed that Steve could stay in the loft for a few more months so he could have the chance to look for another place to live in the summer, when there were more places available.

Lucas had moved into Jill's room, so Steve had been able to take Lucas's. It was workable as a temporary solution but definitely not ideal.

Jill wasn't excited about Steve moving out. She would miss him a lot. But she definitely wouldn't complain when these fights finally came to an end.

She did a quick scan of the common room to discover that Lucas wasn't around. He'd texted her that he had a job this afternoon and wasn't sure when he'd be back. She headed to the bedroom after a quick wave at Michelle and saw that Lucas wasn't there either.

She closed the bedroom door and groaned softly as she flopped onto the bed, too tired to even take off her boots.

Work had been stressful lately with another big project on a tight timeline, and she really didn't need to hear this fight on coming home today.

Occasionally she thought about maybe getting a new place. One just with Lucas. There was a lot she liked about that idea.

But she still loved living here. She loved the loft apartment, and she loved Michelle and Steve. Plus she and Lucas had only been seriously dating for six weeks.

She wasn't going to jump the gun.

Her phone chimed, and she picked it up, wondering if it was Lucas.

It wasn't. It was Laura, sending a couple of pictures of the kids.

Smiling, Jill texted back a response.

Laura and the rest of Lucas's family were treating her like she was part of the family now, and Jill didn't mind.

She didn't mind at all.

She was thinking about that and still lying on the bed twenty minutes later when the bedroom door opened. Lucas came in, closing the door behind him.

He wore khakis and gray T-shirt, and he had shaved that morning. He was handsome and masculine and familiar and giving her a look of close scrutiny.

"You okay?" he asked, approaching the bed.

"Yeah." She gave him a tired smile. "Just tired. They were fighting when I got home."

His face relaxed, and he lowered himself to the bed beside her. Unlike her, he toed his shoes off before he did. "They must have retreated to their separate corners now since neither of them were around."

She turned her head to look at him. "Good."

He reached over to take her hand, rubbing her palm with his thumb. "You sure you're okay?"

"Tired. I'm glad you're here."

"I'm glad I'm here too." He was still caressing her hand, and it was generating all kinds of pleasant sensations. Not just in her hand but running through her whole body.

"How was your job?"

"Good. Just tax prep. Nothing too complicated. What about you? Is Patrick being obnoxious again?"

"No. He's trying to be good. It's just a lot to do." She let out a sigh and turned on her side to face Lucas. "I shouldn't complain. I love my job."

"I know you do. But you can complain to me about anything you want."

She smiled at him, scooting over to kiss him gently on the mouth.

To her surprise, he took her head in his hands and deepened the kiss.

She was feeling affectionate rather than sexy, but she didn't mind his urgency, even when he rolled her over onto her back and moved on top of her.

"I guess working on taxes makes you hot," she murmured against his lips when she felt hard evidence of his arousal rubbing against her hip.

"Definitely." He straightened up and reached down to unzip one of her boots.

She smiled with warm leisure as he pulled both of them off.

His eyes were hot as he gazed down at her body, and she felt the deepest combination of responses to his look—feeling both desired and loved.

"I love you," she whispered.

His eyes moved to her face, and his expression softened as he met her eyes. "I love you too. So much."

"So much." She reached for him to pull him down into another kiss.

After he'd kissed her, he lifted his head a few inches, still so close she could feel his breath. "I was thinking…"

"What were you thinking about?"

"I don't want to leave Michelle in a lurch or anything."

Her breath hitched as she started to follow this line of thought.

Lucas continued, "But it might be nice to live just with you."

A warm wave of joy washed over her. "That would be nice. Not right away though. It's already hard enough for Michelle with the breakup. But maybe Chloe could move back in here in a few months, now that she's finally found a better job."

He nodded. "That's what I was thinking. Maybe at the end of the summer, when there are a lot of places on the market."

"Yes," she breathed. "I'd love that. We can still hang out with the others a lot."

"Definitely." He kissed her again. "And maybe we could think about some other things."

It was too much—too close to what she'd been secretly dreaming about. Her eyes widened. "What things?" she rasped.

"Other things." He was smiling as he kissed her again. "I can wait. I don't want to push too much or go too fast. I know we haven't been together for very long. But I'm serious about being your forever man, and I'd kind of like it to be official."

His voice was almost sheepish, and a quick look at his face revealed that he was slightly nervous and trying to hide it.

He was nervous. Which meant he was serious.

He was serious.

The joy swept over her, warming her cheeks, tightening in her throat. She managed to say, "I'm not in a hurry either, but whenever you're ready, I'll be ready too."

She saw the acknowledgment of her words pass over his face. She saw the quick flash of something deeper than joy, something bigger than happiness. But all he said was, "Good. I'm glad to hear that."

He kissed her again, and she kissed him back, and they made love right there on top of the covers, without even taking off their clothes. It was deep and full and eager to the point of clumsiness.

It was what Jill had always wanted. Love. Roots. The beginnings of a family. It hadn't happened the way she'd thought it would. It was harder and slower and messier—built on need and tears as much as desire and laughter.

But she wouldn't have had it any other way.

About Noelle Adams

Noelle handwrote her first romance novel in a spiral-bound notebook when she was twelve, and she hasn't stopped writing since. She has lived in eight different states and currently resides in Virginia, where she writes full time, reads any book she can get her hands on, and offers tribute to a very spoiled cocker spaniel.

She loves travel, art, history, and ice cream. After spending far too many years of her life in graduate school, she has decided to reorient her priorities and focus on writing contemporary romances. For more information, please check out her website: noelle-adams.com.

Books by Noelle Adams

Trophy Husbands
> Part-Time Husband
> Practice Husband

The Loft Series
> Living with Her One-Night Stand
> Living with Her Ex-Boyfriend
> Living with Her Fake Fiancé

One Fairy Tale Wedding Series
> Unguarded
> Untouched
> Unveiled

Accidental Bride

Heirs of Damon Series
Seducing the Enemy
Playing the Playboy
Engaging the Boss
Stripping the Billionaire

Willow Park Series
Married for Christmas
A Baby for Easter
A Family for Christmas
Reconciled for Easter
Home for Christmas

One Night Novellas
One Night with her Best Friend
One Night in the Ice Storm
One Night with her Bodyguard
One Night with her Boss
One Night with her Roommate
One Night with the Best Man

The Protectors Series (co-written with Samantha Chase)
Protecting his Best Friend's Sister
Protecting the Enemy
Protecting the Girl Next Door
Protecting the Movie Star

Standalones
A Negotiated Marriage

Listed
Bittersweet
Missing
Revival
Holiday Heat
Salvation
Excavated
Overexposed
Road Tripping
Chasing Jane
Late Fall
Fooling Around
Married by Contract
Trophy Wife
Bay Song
Her Reluctant Billionaire
Second Best

Made in the USA
Columbia, SC
04 July 2018